4 A STEVIE DIAMOND MYSTERY

How can a frozen detective stay hot on the trail?

LINDA BAILEY

KIDS CAN PRESS LTD.
TORONTO

Kids Can Press Ltd. acknowledges with appreciation the assistance of the Canada Council and the Ontario Arts Council in the production of this book.

Canadian Cataloguing in Publication Data
Bailey, Linda, 1948–
How can a frozen detective stay hot on the trail?
(A Stevie Diamond mystery ; 4)
ISBN 1-55074-321-X

1. Title. II. Series.

PS8553.A3644H6 1996 jC813'.54 C96-930722–5
PZ7.B35Ho 1996

Kids Can Press Ltd.
29 Birch Avenue
Toronto, Ontario, Canada
M4V 1E2

Edited by Charis Wahl
Interior designed by Tom Dart/First Folio Resource Group, Inc.
Printed and bound in Canada
Text stock contains over 50% recycled paper

Many thanks to Katherine Zmetana, who suggested the idea of a carnivorous plants theft; to Doug Fung, who gave me a tour of his plant collection; and to Charis Wahl, who not only did a great editing job, but also came up with the title.

96 0 9 8 7 6 5 4 3 2 1

For Connie and Lorne Grainger,
two of the readingest (and nicest) people I know

CHAPTER

A GOOD DETECTIVE, I FIGURE, SHOULD BE ABLE TO *smell* trouble coming. Most of the time I have a pretty good nose for it. But this time? Not a whiff. Not until Jesse and I were practically in Winnipeg. Even then, he had to tell me.

"What kind of trouble?" I said, jerking up straight in my plane seat.

Jesse shrugged. "I'm not sure. But Misha sounded really upset on the phone last night, Stevie. I think he was … crying."

Crying? A sixteen-year-old guy?

Must be *big* trouble.

I glanced out the window. Just snow-covered prairie below. In half an hour, Jesse and I would be landing in Winnipeg for a New Year's holiday. Waiting for us would be his grandma and his sixteen-year-old uncle.

Misha. The one with the trouble.

I'm Stevie Diamond. Stevie, short for Stephanie. Twelve going on thirteen. I live in Vancouver, a few doors from Jesse, which makes us neighbours *and* friends. Detective partners, too, ever since we accidentally stumbled into a couple of mysteries together. Diamond & Kulniki, that's us. Back home in Vancouver, we're famous.

Well, okay. Maybe not exactly famous. But we *have* been in the newspaper a couple of times. Front page.

I peered out the tiny window again, looking for Winnipeg. Still flat, white and empty out there. Nothing but telephone poles, thin grey roads and, once in a while, a farmhouse with a few buildings scattered around.

Beside me, Jesse bit his lip nervously. "I hope this trouble of Misha's doesn't spoil our holiday. He's got a car, and I was hoping he could take us places. Tobogganing and skating and stuff." He stopped. "Hey, Stevie, do you think the trouble could be, like … a girlfriend or something?"

A girlfriend? Now that could put a glitch into my plans. I had my own ideas for Misha, and they had nothing to do with tobogganing.

It had all started with the magazines. A few months before, I had moved up to the teenage section of the library. One day I found a bunch of magazines with names like *Teen Scene* and *Teen Personality*. All of them – every single one – had huge articles on flirting. The Number One Skill, one magazine called it. Seemed like if you didn't know how to flirt, you might as well just skip teenage life – move straight on to becoming a parent or teacher or something.

One of the magazines even had a quiz. It was called "Test Your Flirting Power." The best score you could get was 35.

Anything less than eight and you were a Lame Loser.

Know what I got?

Three.

Pathetic. I hadn't even made it into Dating Duds.

"Don't give up hope," said the magazine. "Maybe all you need is practice."

I thought it over. Maybe the magazine was right. After all, when had I ever had a chance? I couldn't practise on Jesse – he was my buddy. And most of the guys in my class were only interested in sports. They wouldn't recognize a flirt if it hit them over the head.

Then I remembered Misha. Sixteen years old. Perfect. Ten days in Winnipeg. Perfect. I'd seen a picture of him, and he was cute but not *perfectly* cute, if you know what I mean. Perfect.

I'd been reading those magazines for weeks now, and I figured I was ready. By the time I got home, I should *at least* be in Borderline Babes.

A flight attendant came by, picking up blankets and headsets. Scooping up the wrappings from the extra peanuts Jesse and I had asked for, he gave us a smile.

"Have you been to Winnipeg before?"

I shook my head. "This is my first big trip." Just my luck to have all my relatives living in Vancouver. Every other kid in my school got to fly all sorts of places, visiting.

"I was born in Winnipeg," Jesse told him proudly. "Lived there till I was five."

"Ah," said the flight attendant, nodding. "So you'll be ready."

"Ready for what?" I asked.

"The weather," he said, moving on.

Jesse rolled his eyes. "See? I told you."

"Oh, for crying out loud, Jesse. It snows in Vancouver, too."

"Sure. Once a year, maybe. And it melts in two days. You've lived by the ocean all your life, Stevie, so you don't know. In the prairies, the snow falls and then it *stays* – for months! And it gets really cold. Especially the week after Christmas."

"You know what? You're starting to sound like my mother."

That shut him up.

Ever since Jesse and I had started planning this trip, my mom had been driving me nuts. You wouldn't believe the stuff she dragged out of the closet – moth-eaten scarves, scratchy wool socks, even long red underwear. You'd think I was going to the North Pole.

Jesse muttered something.

"What?" I said.

"You shouldn't have left that jacket behind."

I shook my head. "I am *not* going to show up in Winnipeg looking like a human pillow."

The jacket was this old-lady ski jacket, stuffed full of goose feathers. My mom had insisted on packing it in my suitcase, but I'd managed to dump it in the back of the car on the way to the airport. I'd also unloaded a few other things, including the Frankenstein boots. They were made of heavy rubber lined with thick felt and were so wide they were practically square. When I walked around the kitchen in them, I clunked.

Looking down at the arriving-in-Winnipeg outfit *I* had picked out, I couldn't help smiling. Great-looking jean jacket with beads all over the front. Faded jeans. Black ankle boots. If the quiz in *Teen Personality* had been on clothes, I would have gotten at least a 30.

Jesse, on the other hand, looked like a polar bear. He was stuffed into a thick white sweater with a turtleneck that came up over his ears. His boots were so heavy he'd had to shuffle onto the plane.

"Well, don't say I didn't warn you," he warned me.

"I won't."

"It's your funeral."

"I know."

"Don't say I didn't try."

"Okay."

"Because if you're not going to listen – "

"Jesse, will you *forget* about my clothes?"

"Ladies and gentlemen," said a voice over the intercom, "we are now beginning our final descent into Winnipeg."

Jesse started waving while we were still on the airport escalator. "There they are! Hey, Bobbi! Misha!"

Suddenly, he was off the escalator and grabbed by a small, sandy-haired woman with dangling golden earrings and a wide smile. She was wearing wool pants, a purple toque and a puffy red jacket that looked a lot like the one I'd dumped.

It was Jesse's grandma – he called her Bobbi because their family came from Ukraine, and in Ukrainian the word for grandmother is *baba*. When Jesse was a baby, it came out Bobbi instead. Pretty soon everyone was calling her Bobbi.

"Jesse Kulniki, you gorgeous thing! Am I glad to see you!" She gave him a rib-squeezing hug. "Look at you! You're taller than me."

Then she spotted me and grinned.

"Are you Stevie?" I got a hug, too, but not such a squeezy one. "Welcome to Winnipeg!"

Jesse's eyes suddenly lit up. "MISHA!" he hollared.

Okay, there he was.

My flirt target.

Taller than me. Sort of on the skinny side, like Jesse. Thick hair, dark blond, a bit long. Zit on the chin, but only a small one. Green eyes, wire-rimmed glasses. Sensitive-looking.

Perfect.

I gave him my most enthusiastic smile.

Which he ignored.

Okay. Well, there was plenty of time.

"Hey, kid!" he said, giving Jesse a half-hearted punch on the arm.

That's all. Just "Hey, kid!"

Jesse punched him back. Then Misha walked away. Without a smile. Without a word. Without even a *hi* to me. Jesse glanced over at Bobbi, who just shook her head.

"Let him be," she said. "I'll explain later."

We followed her to the luggage carousels, answering a bunch of questions about our flight and our families and the weather in Vancouver. Misha didn't show up again until we were hauling our suitcases off the moving belt. He had a slumpy look.

I watched him out of the corner of my eye. It didn't *have* to be girl trouble, did it? Maybe he'd just gotten a lousy report card.

We all stood around, waiting, while Jesse did his Arctic survival routine. First, he hauled on a red toque and a down jacket. Then he wrapped a thick scarf around his head three times, covering his mouth and nose. Finally, he pulled on two pairs of mitts. Bobbi grinned. Even Misha managed a half-smile.

As we headed for the door, Bobbi turned to me. "Where's your coat, Stevie? It's pretty chilly out there today."

I groaned. Not her, too.

"Listen, Mrs. Kulniki – "

"Call me Bobbi."

"Okay. Bobbi. I wish you and everybody else would stop worrying. I happen to have this really high body temperature, see? I don't feel the cold."

"Are you sure? The way you're dressed – "

"Honest!" I said, stepping through the automatic door behind Misha. "I don't see why everybody is making such a big deal about – "

CHAPTER 2

C-C-C-C-COOOLLLLD!!!!!

I gasped.

Tried to gasp.

Like breathing ice.

"Stevie? Are you all right?"

Freezing blast on face, chest, legs. Hnnnnnh ...

"She's not moving. Stevie!"

Hair lifted by icy, shrieking wind.

"Say something."

Mouth, jaws, nose, slamming shut, frozen. Hnnnhhhhh ...

"For goodness' sake, Jesse, help me pull her along. She's stiff as a board. Stevie, can you at least move your feet?"

"I warned her, Bobbi. She can't say I didn't warn her."

"Never mind that, Jesse. Just grab that arm and pull."

Dragged through whirling, biting snow. Icy needles stabbing cheeks. Freezing gusts howling through armpits.

"Oh good. Here's the car. Quick, Misha, turn the heat on. Help me get her into the back seat, Jesse. You'll have to bend her at the waist."

Shoved like frozen turkey into car. Whonk! Head hit door. Hnnnnnh ...

"Turn the heat up full blast, Misha. Let's see, there's an old sleeping bag back here somewhere. Help me wrap it around her, Jesse. Stevie, can you speak now?"

"Mnnnnnnn ..."

"That's a start," said Bobbi.

"I warned her," muttered Jesse. "Over and over, I told her about the cold. But would she listen? Oh no, she knew everything. I hate to say I told you so, but – "

I could move my eyeballs now. I shot Jesse a filthy look.

"Gbbbbbbbzzzzz!"

"I bet she's got hypothermia." He sounded pleased. "We learned about it in school. Your whole body slows down – your heart, your brain. You can *die* of hypothermia."

"Rrrrzzzzzzz!" I snarled. "Ffrrlllll!"

"She'll be fine." Bobbi was rubbing my arms with both hands. "Look! She can already wiggle her fingers."

Jesse wiped off the window and peered outside. Snow flew at the car in noisy blasts. "Nasty out there," he said, "even for someone like me, who's used to it."

Bobbi nodded. "It's minus thirty. But it was the wind-chill factor that got to Stevie."

"The wind-chill factor?" I said. Unfortunately, my jaws were still locked together. It came out, "Zzz wddd-chhhhh fzzzrrrr?"

Bobbi explained. "Well, minus thirty is very cold. But the strong wind we have today makes it feel even colder. We call that the wind-chill factor."

It took a while, but as the car warmed up, the frozen turkey finally started to thaw. My jaws came loose, and my teeth started to chatter.

"How do you s-stand it?" I asked Bobbi. "The c-c-cold?"

"It's no problem at all if you're dressed for it. Honestly, Stevie, I don't understand how your parents could send you off this way. This jacket! These boots!"

"Well, you can't really blame my parents," I muttered, not looking at Jesse. "After all, they grew up in Vancouver. They don't understand cold."

"Never mind. As soon as we get you home, we'll dress you properly. You won't even notice the cold. Right, Misha?"

Misha was alone in the front seat and didn't answer. I glanced around. In Vancouver, we'd call this kind of car a junker – seats all caved in, upholstery ripped, cracks in the windows.

Bobbi leaned over and whispered in my ear. "This is Misha's first car. He calls it Old Pete, and he's very proud of it. I thought he'd want to show it off to you and Jesse."

From what I could see, Misha didn't look interested in showing anything to anybody. Hunched over the steering wheel, he peered squinty-eyed into the flying snow. At a stop sign, Old Pete sputtered as if it was going to stall. Misha leaned over and gave the dashboard a pat.

It was a long ride. The streets were like half-tunnels, with high snowbanks on each side. Ice streaked the pavement, and when we stopped at lights, people rushed past, bundled in scarves, mitts and heavy coats. Christmas lights blinked through the whirling snow – red, green, yellow, blue.

Soon we were leaving the city, driving along an open country highway. Jesse had told me that Bobbi and Misha lived on the outskirts of Winnipeg, on a small farm, where they grew vegetables. They had a huge greenhouse, too, where they grew houseplants all year round.

"How much farther?" I asked.

"Not far," said Bobbi. "Maybe fifteen minutes."

Snow hit the windows in even more furious gusts now, but inside Old Pete, we were as warm and snug as that bug you always hear about. The one in the rug. My eyes dropped shut, and I almost dozed off.

It wasn't until the car stopped that I realized – I'd have to get *out*.

No way.

"Come on, Stevie." Jesse grabbed my arm. "It's just a few steps to the door. We'll run."

Run? Oh sure. But Bobbi and Misha were already opening their doors.

Okay. No choice.

I stepped out.

Gasped.

Frozen turkey! C-C-C-COLD! Run!!!

There was a horrible moment at the door as Bobbi fiddled with the frozen lock. I turned my back to the wind and, in between bone-jolting shivers, got my first good look at the outside of Old Pete. A junker all right – mostly lime green, except for its fenders, which were white, and the front hood, which was a bright blood red.

Misha saw me looking.

"N-n-nice c-c-carrr," I said.

How are you supposed to flirt when your lips are frozen?

Bobbi's house – thank goodness – was toasty warm.

"Come into the living room," she said. "I've made a little snack."

She hustled us into a room with a thick beige carpet and pale pink furniture. Lots of little knick-knacky, ornament things on tables – the kind that get knocked over easily. It was totally neat, like Jesse's house in Vancouver. Not a speck of dust, not a newspaper lying around, not a single, solitary sock under the couch. The kind of place where I was really going to have to watch myself.

Bobbi's "little snack" was on the coffee table. She whisked the wrappings off a giant plate of sandwiches, a bowl of dill pickles, and a platter of desserts – shortbread cookies, fruitcake and my all-time favourite, lemon meringue tarts.

"Jesse is here so seldom that I like to spoil him when I get the chance," she said. "I can see you've got your eye on those lemon tarts, Stevie. Help yourself. I'll go make some hot cider."

Jesse headed for the bathroom, and I sat down next to the food. Misha plopped down on a couch across from me. As I reached for a tart, I got this funny feeling – like he was watching me. I looked up. He *was* watching me.

Perfect.

I decided to start with a Significant Glance. According to *Teens Alive,* all you had to do was raise your eyebrows a tiny bit and widen your eyes.

I tried it.

Misha's eyes widened, too. Was he giving me a Significant Glance back?

Maybe I should try the Eye Lock. It sounded easy – you just had to keep your eyes glued to his. I could do that.

I did.

Not as easy as it sounds. Misha's eyes started darting all over the room. Fortunately, they kept darting back to me. Good. After about thirty seconds his left cheek started to twitch. They hadn't mentioned twitching in *Teens Alive,* but I figured it was probably okay. I gave him another Significant Glance.

He made a strange sound. If I didn't know better, I would have called it a yelp.

Suddenly he leaped to his feet and stumbled towards the door. After slamming into Jesse, he pushed past to where Bobbi was just rounding a corner with a tray of hot cider.

Misha nearly knocked it right out of her hands.

CHAPTER

3

Wow!

This flirting was powerful stuff.

"What happened?" Jesse stared, amazed, over his shoulder.

Setting her tray down on a coffee table, Bobbi shook her head. "Misha's a little jumpy these days. He's – well, he's in a bit of trouble."

Jesse and I exchanged looks.

"What kind of trouble?" Jesse asked.

She sighed. "Trouble with the police."

The police? I was right. Serious trouble.

"I was going to tell you later, after you'd had a chance to get settled," said Bobbi. "You see, Misha has been involved with this club for a while now – a horticultural club."

"Horti-who?" said Jesse.

"Horticulture," I repeated. "That's plants."

Bobbi nodded.

"So this is a gardening club?" I asked, reaching for a mug of cider.

"Well, sort of," said Bobbi. "You see, the members

of this club raise a certain *kind* of plant. Some people think these plants are a little peculiar."

"How could a plant be peculiar?" asked Jesse. "Plants are great. They make oxygen for us to breathe. They – "

"Carnivorous plants," said Bobbi.

"Carni-who?" said Jesse.

"Carnivorous," I repeated. "You know. Meat-eating."

Jesse turned pale. "You mean . . . no! Misha? My uncle Misha? Raising meat-eating plants?"

Our eyes widened as we both had the same sick-making thought. Jesse looked like he was going to faint.

It was up to me to ask. "Bobbi, are you trying to tell us that Misha raised a carnivorous plant, and it . . . it *ate* somebody?"

"What???" Bobbi burst out laughing. "Gosh, what a thought!" She kept on laughing – for longer than necessary, in my opinion. It wasn't *that* strange an idea.

"These plants don't eat *people,*" she explained. "They eat insects. Oh, I think in hot, tropical areas, they can sometimes grow quite large. Misha says they can get big enough to digest a small animal. A mouse, for instance. Or a bird. Even a small monkey. But people? No!"

"Birds?" said Jesse in a tiny, high voice. "They eat birds?" He looked even sicker.

There are two things you probably ought to know about Jesse. One, he loves birds. He watches them through binoculars, collects books about them, feeds them in the winter – the whole bit. And two, he's a vegetarian. The idea of eating meat makes him sick. I could just imagine how he felt about a *plant* that eats meat.

A plant that eats *birds,* yet!

"The club is called the Carnivore Club," Bobbi continued. "Misha joined it three months ago. I was so pleased. He's such a bright boy – the youngest member the club has ever had. He got very involved, too, especially when they started planning their exhibition at the Winnipeg Conservatory."

Jesse opened his mouth, but before he could say "conserva-who," Bobbi explained. "The Winnipeg Conservatory is this huge indoor greenhouse where they display all kinds of rare plants. It's absolutely beautiful. Anyway, the Conservatory people asked the club if they would bring in their best plants for an exhibition. They're calling it 'Carnivores!' The show is supposed to open on January 7."

"Supposed to open?" said Jesse. "You mean, it's not going to?"

"No," replied a voice from behind me. "And everyone is blaming me."

I turned. Misha was leaning in the doorway, a lock of blond hair hanging over his eyes. He pushed it back with his hand and glanced in my direction. Ready maybe for another round of flirting?

Well, he'd have to wait. The minute I heard the word "police," the flirt in me took a dive, and the detective took over. I *had* to hear the rest of this story.

Bobbi continued, her voice soft. "The club was trying to work out how to display the plants. They decided that the members should bring all their best plants together before the exhibition so they could see what they'd look like."

"At Muffy's house," said Misha.

"Muffy De Witt," said Bobbi. "She's a member of the club, lives right near here. Anyway, that's what they did. Everyone took their best plants to Muffy's house for a big meeting. They were planning to have another meeting the next day."

"Unfortunately," said Misha, "some jerk broke into Muffy's house that night and stole the plants. And everybody thinks *I'm* the jerk!"

"Not everybody." Bobbi's voice was quiet but firm.

I shook my head. "Wait a minute, I don't get it. Why the police? It's just a bunch of plants, right?"

Misha snorted. "These are not just a bunch of plants! They're extremely rare specimens. Some of them are worth thousands of dollars. Others are almost impossible to get."

Bobbi nodded. "That's why the police think it must have been a member of the club. Only the most valuable plants disappeared. It would take an expert to know which ones to steal."

"But why Misha?" asked Jesse. "Why don't they suspect the other members?"

Misha shrugged. "I'm new. I'm young. I'm broke."

"The real problem," said Bobbi, "is the car."

"What car?" Jesse asked.

"Muffy's neighbours saw a car drive up to her house," said Bobbi. "They described it to the police. It was – " She stopped. Glanced at Misha.

"Go ahead, Mom, say it! Lime green. With white fenders. And a red hood."

"Oh!" Jesse and I said it at the same time. There couldn't be *two* cars like that in Winnipeg.

A moment of silence. Then I asked a hard question. "*Were* you there that night, Misha? *Did* you drive over to Muffy's house? Maybe for some other reason?"

"No!" Misha's voice was hoarse. "I was here alone all evening, listening to music. Mom was out at a Christmas party, so she can't back me up. But I didn't go anywhere. I swear it!"

In the even longer silence that followed, my mind did a few quick leaps. But it kept coming back to the same place – things did *not* look good for Misha. I could see why the police suspected him.

"What about Muffy?" I asked. "Where was she?"

"Asleep," said Misha.

"You're kidding," said Jesse. "She slept through her house being robbed?"

Misha grunted. "You'd understand if you saw Muffy's house."

"It's huge," said Bobbi. "A mansion. Muffy lives there on her own."

Misha nodded. "At the meeting that day, Muffy told us she'd been so excited about the exhibit, she couldn't sleep. She blabbed on and on about how she was going to take a sleeping pill and go to bed early. Everyone heard her. Anybody could have turned up that night. Anybody!"

"Anybody in the *club,*" said Jesse.

I tried again. "Didn't the neighbours see any other cars that night?"

Bobbi shook her head. "On these little country roads, people notice every car that goes by. The

neighbours only saw one. The one that – [illegible]
like Old Pete."

Oh, sure, I thought. Of course Bobbi [illegible]
believe her son was innocent. But did [illegible]
believe the roads were jammed with three-coloured junkers like Old Pete?

Jesse cleared his throat. "Well, um, at least Misha is still here. At least, he's not not … uh, you know …"

"Arrested?" said Misha. "Stick around. The police questioned me today for the third time. It was like on TV – they actually told me not to leave town. The way things are going, pretty soon you'll have to visit me in jail."

"Oh, Misha, no!" Bobbi reached a hand in Misha's direction. Suddenly his face got all crumpled-looking. He turned and bolted. A moment later, a door slammed down the hall.

Bobbi clutched Jesse's hand instead. "Jesse, honey, I am *so* glad you're here. I just know you'll be able to make sense out of this mess and help your uncle Misha."

"Me?" Jesse jerked upright.

"Of course, you. Who else? Oh, Jesse, I've been so proud of you." She turned to me. "I guess you know, Stevie, that my grandson here is a brilliant detective. He keeps phoning and writing from Vancouver to tell me about it. Amazing, isn't it? Whenever the police are stumped, they turn to him – a twelve-year-old boy. Of course, Jesse *does* always figure it out for them. A regular Sherlock Holmes!"

I glanced at Jesse, who was suddenly extremely busy examining his socks. "Uh, Bobbi," he said in a oice you could hardly hear, "I, um, well, Stevie here … uh, gave me a hand."

Bobbi's eyebrows rose, and she gave me a beaming smile. "Did she, now? Well, isn't that nice. I suppose all great detectives need assistants. Even Sherlock Holmes had a helper – what's his name, the simple-minded one? Oh yes, Watson."

I bit my lip. Hard.

"Well, that's wonderful," Bobbi went on. "Stevie can *help* you find out who really stole those plants. There's a Carnivore Club meeting tomorrow night. Misha doesn't want to go. He thinks the other members all suspect him. But I told him that's all the more reason why he *should* go – to show he's innocent. If you two go with him, I know he'll feel better. And, Jesse dear, it will give you a chance to poke around and question people and, um, whatever else you do to solve crimes."

Bobbi looked at Jesse with such hope in her eyes that there was only one answer possible.

"Uh … sure," he muttered. "We'll see what we can do."

Letting out a sigh, Bobbi started gathering up the dishes. "I'm so glad. Now you two stay right there while I tidy up. You probably want to, er, discuss strategies."

"Good idea," I said, fixing my eyes on the top of Jesse's head. He was being careful not to look at me. "We'll discuss strategies. I can't wait to find out what Sherlock here has got planned."

CHAPTER 4

I WAITED UNTIL SHE WAS OUT OF THE ROOM. "*WHAT* have you been telling your grandmother?"

Jesse didn't answer at first. Too busy picking lint off his socks. "Nothing much," he said finally.

"What do you mean – nothing much! She thinks you're Sherlock Holmes. She thinks you solved all those mysteries by yourself."

Pulling the sock halfway off his foot, he wound the toe part around his middle finger. "It was long distance, Stevie. You can't expect me to tell her every little detail."

"Little detail!" I was mad enough to spit. "Me? A little detail?" I couldn't believe it! If it hadn't been for me, Jesse would never have become a detective in the first place. He'd still be reading bird books in his bedroom. He'd still be leaping three feet in the air every time he heard a strange noise.

Come to think of it, he *was* still leaping three feet in the air every time he heard a strange noise.

"Bobbi knew I had a partner," muttered Jesse. "At least, she *should* have known. I sent her all the newspaper articles with both our names in them. But I guess I probably told her I was … you know … the main detective."

I glared.

"Well, geez, Stevie, what do you expect me to tell her? That *I* help *you?*"

"Why not? It's the truth!"

He pulled his sock back on. "Now, wait just a minute. Maybe when we started out. But on our last case, who did the rescuing? Who got you out of that cellar you were trapped in?"

"Okay," I admitted, "so you rescued me. But that was just one teensy-weensy, itsy-bitsy moment in the whole case. Compared to what *I* did, it was like a fly speck!"

"Oh, yeah?"

"Yeah!"

We spent the next five minutes arguing about our old cases – who had done what and when and how often and how brilliantly. I won't bore you with the details.

Finally Jesse sighed. "What about Misha?"

Right. Misha. It didn't take a genius to see how serious his problem was. And it *was* pretty flattering that Bobbi had turned to us. The truth is, this was the first time anyone had actually *asked* us to take a case. All that stuff Jesse had told his grandmother about the police asking for our help – that was hooey. Usually adults told us to butt out, as if there was some invisible age requirement for being a detective and we were about ten years too young. It was nice to be taken seriously for a change.

"Are we going to do it?" asked Jesse. "Take the case?"

I nodded.

"It looks bad, doesn't it? For Misha, I mean."

I nodded again. But bad wasn't the word I would have chosen. Dismal, maybe. Hopeless.

"We'll do our best," I said. But a twinge of nervousness fluttered through my stomach. Sure, Jesse and I had had a few successes. But we weren't *really* professional detectives.

Would our best be good enough to keep Misha Kulniki out of jail?

The next morning, with hot waffles on the table and sunlight pouring through the kitchen window, things looked brighter, and I was ready to jump right into detecting. But Misha had gone out for groceries, and there wasn't much we could do without him. After we'd stuffed ourselves with waffles, Jesse offered to show me the greenhouse.

"Not until we get Stevie some warm clothes!" said Bobbi. She disappeared and returned a few minutes later with her arms full. I could see right away that I'd made a big mistake leaving my mom's stuff in Vancouver.

"Now here's a parka Misha used to wear in grade eight. I wonder how he got that awful rip down the front. It's a little grubby, I guess, but it's warm. And here are some ski pants I bought on sale and never wore. Orange isn't really my colour."

I stared at the pile – toques, scarves, thick mitts. "You're kidding! All that stuff just to cross the yard?"

Bobbi laughed. "If you want to spend any time outside, Stevie, you *will* have to dress for it."

Remembering that frozen-turkey feeling, I shuddered. I picked up the orange pants and held them against me.

"They're, um, nice," said Jesse. "Really ... colourful!"

Minutes later, dressed like an Arctic explorer, I was following Jesse and Bobbi down the shovelled path to the greenhouse. It was probably the brightest day I'd ever seen – the sky turquoise blue and the sunlight glaring off the snow so white-bright it made my eyes water. I sucked in air that was cold but not quite as freezing as the night before.

Just as I started to feel the chill, we stepped into the greenhouse. Winter to summer in three steps. The air was suddenly as sweet, warm and moist as a morning in June. All around me was green – bright green, dark green, pale green. Long wooden tables covered in plants.

"It's all houseplants now," said Bobbi, walking down a row of tables. "We sell them to stores around the city. Later, in the spring, this whole place will be full of bedding plants – tiny flowers and vegetables getting a headstart before it warms up enough to plant them in the garden."

Jesse and I followed her, stripping off parkas, mitts and hats. Life in Winnipeg, I could see, was going to involve a whole bunch of putting clothes on and taking them off.

"How do you keep it so warm in here?" I asked.

"Well, the sun helps, of course," said Bobbi, pointing at the sunlight pouring through the roof and walls. "But we have a gas furnace, too." She nodded towards a big square metal thing at the far end. "The heat from that furnace goes up into the ceiling, which is two layers of soft plastic. We heat the air between them."

"Hey, Stevie, check this out." Jesse was pointing at what looked like the longest, fattest balloon in the world. It was made of soft, see-through plastic and stretched under a row of tables that went from one end of the greenhouse to the other. Kind of like a soft, puffy snake filled with air. Looking around, I could see that all the tables had long snake-balloons underneath them.

"That's how we distribute the warm air inside here and make sure it's even," said Bobbi. "Those tubes are hooked up to the furnace. You can see the holes in them where the warm air comes out."

I touched a hole about as big as my fist in one of the balloons. Warm air tickled my fingers. I could see why the plants looked so happy.

"Neat!" I said.

For the next hour or so, Jesse and I helped Bobbi in the greenhouse. We moved plants out of tiny pots into bigger pots, watered things and picked dead leaves off some of the older plants. It was a nice place to work, especially when the world outside was frozen solid.

Jesse was repotting a plant when suddenly he snatched his hand away as if it had been burnt.

"Wait a minute! Are any of these plants carn – carn – you know!"

Bobbi smiled. "Carnivorous? No. Misha likes to keep a close eye on his plants. He has grow-lights in his bedroom and keeps them in there."

Jesse turned pale. "In his bedroom? The room I'm *sleeping* in?"

Bobbi nodded. "Didn't you see them?"

"Well, uh, sure, I noticed some, uh, plants, but I didn't know what *kind* of – "

"Now, Jesse, those plants wouldn't hurt a fly!" When Bobbi realized what she'd said, she burst out laughing. I cracked up, too. Jesse stared at us in horror.

"Well, I guess they *would* hurt a fly," corrected Bobbi, "but they won't hurt you, so stop worrying. Go on outside now and get some fresh air."

Jesse was still muttering as we trudged out. "How can I *sleep* in that room, Stevie? With innocent insects dying all around me? It'll be like sleeping in a slaughterhouse."

Fortunately, all it took to get his mind off the carnivorous plants was a couple of well-aimed snowballs. He tossed a few back, and soon we were having an all-out snowball fight. Jesse was quicker, but I had better aim. After that, we tried to build an igloo, but the blocks wouldn't stick and kept falling in on us. Jesse said he'd find a book that told how to do it.

I learned a few things about cold that day. I learned that it attacks your nose first, freezing all those little hairs inside and tightening up your nostrils. Before you know it, your nose has turned Rudolph red and started running. *Not* attractive. Then, because your nose is plugged, you end up breathing cold air through your mouth. Makes your teeth feel like you've been chomping on ice cream.

I also discovered that Bobbi was right – the cold isn't so bad if you're dressed for it. The worst I suffered was a few tingling toes and fingers. By the time we went inside, I felt like a real prairie girl – tough, hardy, outdoorsy, able to handle anything the weather could throw at me.

"That was great," I told Jesse as we took off our jackets.

"You bet!" he said. "Next time we'll stay out longer. Maybe a whole half hour."

Our smiles faded as we heard Misha's voice.

"I'm not going to that meeting, Mom. You don't know what it's like. They think I ruined the exhibit. They *hate* me!"

Jesse and I stared at each other.

Playtime was over.

Work had begun.

CHAPTER

It took Bobbi two hours to persuade Misha to go to the Carnivore Club meeting.

It took two seconds at Muffy's house to see why he hadn't wanted to go. Two seconds of silence, stares, even a few gasps, as the twenty or so club members spotted us in the doorway. Standing beside Misha, I felt like Jack the Ripper's girlfriend. As more and more seconds crept by in silence, I felt a wild urge to scream, "I'm innocent, do you hear me? Innocent!"

The seconds grew. The silence spread.

My feet felt glued to the door mat.

Finally, a short woman in a baby-blue dress glanced up and almost dropped her teapot. She was one of those chicken-shaped people with plump middles and skinny little legs. She scurried over, her golden curls shaking.

"Oh my! Misha! We – uh – that is – "

"It's okay, Muffy." Misha hunched into his jacket and stared at the floor. "I told my mom this was a bad idea. We won't stick around."

Muffy sighed, her chin trembling. Everyone else stood stiff as statues. Misha turned to go.

He was stopped by a white-haired man, who stepped through the crowd and took his arm. The man's skin was rosy pink, and his mouth and nose curved upwards into an elfish smile.

"Misha, my boy! I was hoping you'd show up. My new nepenthes has been looking peaky, and I'd appreciate your advice."

Muffy's tiny hands fluttered like a couple of birds. She sucked in air two or three times before she could speak. "Why – why yes, of course. Lester's right! You *must* come in, Misha. Why, nothing's been proven – oh dear – I mean, nobody really knows what happened, and – oh dear – "

Before she could oh-dear again, the pink-faced guy – Lester – interrupted. "Looks like you brought some new members." He glanced at Jesse and me. "Do you two raise carnivorous plants?"

Jesse's mouth curled up as if he'd just tasted something bad.

"This is my nephew, Jesse," Misha mumbled. "And his, uh, friend."

"Stevie," I added helpfully. "My name's Stevie Diamond, and I'm *extremely* interested in carnivorous plants."

"My, my," trilled Muffy, her golden curls bobbing. "Do come in then. Yes, absolutely! Have a cup of tea, and – oh dear, do you drink tea? Well, a cookie perhaps, and ..."

With Muffy on one side and Lester on the other, Misha, Jesse and I made our way to the refreshment table. One by one, the other club members went back to their conversations.

"That was close," whispered Jesse. "What do we do now, Stevie?"

"We keep our ears open and our mouths shut. Go mingle in the crowd."

I was about to mingle myself, but I hadn't counted on Muffy, who seemed pretty excited about having someone new to talk to.

"You're probably wondering why I'm called Muffy. I'm not surprised, everybody does. No matter where I go, they say, 'Muffy, what an *interesting* name, how did you get it?' Actually, it's a nickname. When I was a little girl, I was round as a puffball with white, white skin and blue, blue eyes. See?" She stuck her face into mine and blinked. "My daddy said I looked just like a blueberry muffin. It's true, he did! Isn't that cute? So he called me Muffin, and pretty soon everyone called me Muffin, and then it got shortened to Muffy!"

"Interesting," I said. "My real name is Stephanie, and – "

"Poor, dear Misha," she went on. "Other people, well, they've been saying the most *terrible* things, but I can't believe for a moment he did anything wrong, can you? He's the nicest boy, so sweet, and he knows so much about these plants – helps me out no end. I'm still learning, you see. To tell you the truth, I only joined because my cooking club folded. There I was, with all this time on my hands and this great big solarium in my house, and I said to myself, Muffy, you really ought to grow some plants in there! And then I saw this show on TV about carnivorous plants. My dear, they were just so fascinating, and ..."

I felt myself going cross-eyed. It happens every time I get terminally bored. Blinking hard, I glanced around. We were in the biggest kitchen I'd ever seen. You could have played basketball in there. A huge carved wooden table stood at one end, under a fancy chandelier. The other end had the usual kitchen stuff, except that everything was twice as big, new and shiny as normal. The counter gleamed with silver – silver teapot, silver coffee urn, silver creamer, sugar bowl and spoons – and the walls were covered in silver-and-green wallpaper with huge flowers all over it. When I spotted a grand piano and another chandelier through a doorway, I came to my first brilliant detective conclusion: Muffy was rich.

My second brilliant conclusion was that if I didn't get away from her soon, I'd scream. She was starting to tell me about her plans to redecorate her bathrooms – all five of them.

"I was thinking maybe cream-coloured tiles with tiny blue cornflowers for the top bathroom and a peachy sort of shade on the walls and – "

Fortunately, at that moment, a tall woman with huge glasses interrupted. She was wearing a black dress and had skinny arms and legs. I couldn't help thinking of a daddy-long-legs spider. She told Muffy it was time to start the meeting, and we all filed through some rooms full of expensive-looking furniture until we came to one where rows of chairs had been set up. I slipped in beside Jesse and Misha as the spider-woman took her place at the front of the room.

"Who's she?" I whispered.

"Veda Bickel," Misha whispered back. "President of the club. She hates me."

"Why?"

He shrugged.

I glanced around as people settled into their chairs. A perfect opportunity to detect! If Misha hadn't stolen the plants, then it had to be somebody else in this room. Who looked suspicious?

How about that chubby guy in the checked suit – the one with glasses thick as pop bottles, held together over his nose with adhesive tape? I watched as he crossed one white-socked ankle neatly over the other. Nope, forget it. He didn't look daring enough to break into a cardboard box.

Well, how about the big, sloppy guy whose pockets were jammed with ballpoint pens? Noticing me watching, he gave me a cheery wave. Then he let out a loud burp and giggled.

Okay, maybe not.

Next I spotted a quiet little white-haired woman who was biting her fingernails. Must be feeling guilty about something. After watching her for a moment, I decided it was probably an overdue library book.

I glanced sideways. Misha was slouched in his chair, breathing heavily. The muscles in his jaws stood out like Ping-Pong balls, and his wrists were jammed together like they were just waiting for handcuffs. Every few seconds, he glanced nervously around the room.

I sighed. This was going to be even harder than I thought.

The meeting didn't help. Veda Bickel droned on about fees and dues and last year's meetings. I guess I sort of dozed off. When I felt Jesse's elbow in my ribs, I realized that Veda's voice had gotten louder and the last word I'd heard was "robbery." I jerked awake.

"And to think," Veda was saying, eyes flashing behind the huge glasses, "that this crime was probably the work of one of our own members. To think that the thief could be right here among us!" She stared straight at Misha, who, I am sorry to say, slunk down even further in his chair. "Whoever did it should be – " She stopped so we could all finish her sentence in our minds. Boiled in oil, I thought. Fed to the lions. Veda looked *extremely* teed off.

"I'll say no more," she finished with a sniff. "It's in the hands of the police now, and I am certain they will make an arrest very soon. But I would like to remind all of you that when a certain young member wanted to join the club some months ago, I was firmly opposed. Members of this club, I said, should be at least twenty-one years of age. But I was outvoted and – well, I'll say no more."

Misha had sunk so low he was practically on the floor. Personally, I thought it was a dirty trick, talking about "a certain young member." It's like when a teacher talks about "certain people in this class." Everybody knows who it is, but if the teacher doesn't say your name, how can you defend yourself?

Misha could at least try. If he was innocent, why didn't he say something?

Lester stood up, and for a minute I thought *he* was going to defend Misha. But all he did was suggest a visit to Muffy's solarium to check out the plants that were left.

As we got to our feet, Jesse whispered to Misha, "What's Lester all about?"

"A good guy," said Misha. "He owns a flower shop downtown, but his real love is carnivorous plants. He's become an expert. People know Lester Potts all over the world."

"An expert?" said Jesse. "So how come he asked you for advice?"

"He was just being nice. Hey, listen. I don't want to go in there – to the, you know, solarium. I'll wait for you guys in the kitchen." He disappeared.

Jesse shrugged, and he and I followed the crowd through seven or eight more rooms and halls. As we neared the solarium, Jesse whispered, "Scene of the crime, Stevie."

I nodded. "Keep your eyes peeled."

The solarium was a round room with a high glass dome for a roof – warm and damp-smelling, like Bobbi's greenhouse. It was full of plants – the rejects the thief hadn't taken.

We were barely inside the door when Jesse started acting weird – walking stiffly like a robot, arms tight against his sides.

"*What* are you doing?"

"Keep your fingers in, Stevie. Stay in the middle."

"Why?"

"I don't trust them."

"Trust who?"

"Who do you think? The plants, of course!"

"What?!!"

"Well, *look* at them! They're disgusting!"

I looked. Some of the plants *did* have funny, swollen things hanging over the edges of their planters.

Lester Potts must have been standing behind us, listening. "Pitcher plants," he said. "They're named for those hanging parts. See how they're shaped like lemonade pitchers?"

I leaned over to get a better look. Jesse grabbed my arm. What did he think – that I was going to fall in?

"How do they catch insects?" I asked Lester.

He smiled eagerly. "It's ingenious," he said. "Each pitcher is a trap – a marvellous, clever trap. You see this opening at the top? It's coated with sweet nectar. Now just imagine Joe Insect coming along. He spots the nectar and says to himself, 'Hmm, looks pretty tasty.' But when he steps up to taste it, suddenly – whoops! – down he slides, down, down this slippery slope right into the pitcher."

I thought for a second. "Why doesn't Joe Insect just climb back out?"

"Oh, he *tries*. But see? The slope is covered in sharp hairs, and they all point downwards. To poor Joe climbing back up, they're like swords in his face. So down he slides, down, down until he ends up in the soup!"

"The soup?" I repeated. Jesse gulped.

"Digestive enzymes," whispered Lester, with a grin. "Like you have in your mouth and stomach. They dissolve things. Poor Joe is desperate now, still trying to climb that slippery slope. But down near the bottom, the slope is scaly. Little bits of it break off and attach to his feet. Suddenly it's like he's wearing skis! Every time he gets a few steps up – whoosh! – back down he goes. Finally, he's exhausted. He can't take any more. He lies there, struggling feebly, half drowned, in the soup, until he is … slowly … eaten … alive!"

"Nooooo!" groaned Jesse, both hands over his face.

I stared at the nearest pitcher in awe. "Really?"

Lester's eyes shone. "Bit by bit, the soft flesh is eaten off Joe Insect's body – until nothing is left but … the shell."

He gave the pitcher a little pat. "Isn't nature wonderful?"

"Wonderful!!" sputtered Jesse. "What about Joe Insect?"

"Oh," said Lester. "Not very pleasant for him, I suppose."

I glanced around the solarium. "Do all these plants work the same way? Do they all have pitchers?"

"Oh, no." Lester shook his head. "These sundews over here, for example, are quite different." He pointed at some low plants with thin tentacle-things sticking up. The tentacles were reddish and glistening, as if they were covered in dew. I touched one. Jesse gasped.

"Ick!" I said. "It's all sticky."

"Precisely," said Lester. "That's how a sundew works. Joe Insect – or Josephine this time – Josephine comes along, gets attracted by the nectar and flies in for a taste. But as soon as she touches it – "

"Dewed, glued and food!" I said. "Right?"

Jesse winced, but Lester laughed. "Exactly!" he said. "Poor Josephine gets stuck to the tentacle. But that's not all. As she struggles to escape, other tentacles sloooowly bend towards her. The more she struggles, the tighter they curl around her. Finally she's trapped – totally helpless. The digestive juices come oozing out, and before you know it, poor Josephine, like Joe, is –

"Insect soup!" I said. "Cool!"

"I like sundews a lot." Lester smiled at the plant fondly. "But my real favourites are the Venus's-flytraps."

"I've seen one of those!" I told him. "At school! The leaves have little spikes along the edges, right? And they snap together to trap the insect inside?"

"Right!" said Lester, excitedly. "It's like a little cage!"

"Does a flytrap have those juices you talked about?" I asked. "The ones that, you know, dissolve the flesh and – "

"I can't *believe* this!"

Lester and I both turned. Jesse's face was tooth-paste green. I guess we'd forgotten about him.

"You two are actually *enjoying* this!" He wobbled slightly and put out a hand to steady himself. It brushed against a plant that looked like a snake – coiled, hooded, all ready to spring. It even had fangs.

"Aaagghh!" yelled Jesse, snatching his hand back.

"The Darlingtonia californica," murmured Lester. "Also known as the cobra plant."

"I think I'm going to be sick." Jesse lurched out the door.

"Oh dear," said Lester, staring after him.

"He's, er, sensitive," I explained.

I was about to take a closer look at the sundews when I noticed people drifting towards the door. Suddenly I felt a jolt of panic. People were leaving. *We'd* have to leave. Here I was, right at the scene of the crime – and I hadn't done a thing except ooh and aah over some weirdo plants.

Maybe it wasn't too late.

"Uh, Lester?"

"Yes, Stevie?"

"The break-in the other night. Do you know how the thief got in?" How on earth did the thief even *find* this solarium, I wondered. I would have spent a couple of hours just wandering around this huge house.

Lester looked at me curiously, then pointed at a door I hadn't noticed at the far end of the solarium. "That door leads outside. It's hardly ever used, so it was snowed over. The thief made his way around the house, through the snow drifts, and used a crowbar to force that door open. At least, I *think* that's how it happened."

I walked over to get a closer look. Just above the door handle, the wood was shredded-looking – from the crowbar, I guess. I put my face against the glass and peered outside. There was a small overhanging roof above the door with a light shining down from it. A few feet away, I could see deep holes in the snow, where someone had stepped. The thief?

Brainwave time. Where there were foot holes, there must also be footprints – the thief's footprints! I put my hand on the doorknob.

Another hand – right above mine – pushed hard against the door.

Lester's hand.

"What are you doing?" he asked.

"Going outside."

"Why?"

"To see those footprints."

Lester looked out. "Interesting. You'd think that last big snow would have filled those prints in – even with the overhang. I guess the wind was blowing the wrong way."

"Excuse me," I said, reaching for the door.

Lester chuckled. "I wouldn't do that, if I were you. After the robbery, Muffy had a new security system put in. Open that door and you'll set off an alarm that will bring half the police in Winnipeg."

"Oh!" I jerked my hand away.

Lester smiled his elf's grin. "Let's go back to the kitchen. See if Muffy has any more of those cookies."

I couldn't spot either Jesse or Misha in the small circle of people gathered in the kitchen. But Muffy was there – curls flying, mouth chattering, hands fluttering around her face. When she saw me, she rushed over, breathless.

"Oh, Stevie! Oh dear! You're still here?"

I stared back, confused. "Of course. Where's Jesse? And Misha?"

Flutter, flap went the hands as she bounced from one tiny foot to the other. "You mean you – oh dear! Well, Jesse's gone outside to – he said he was going to – to throw up. And Misha, he – Veda said something to him, I don't know what – and he went horribly red and rushed out. He said he – oh dear – he said he was going to turn himself in to the police!"

"What???"

Flutter, flutter, flap. "They're gone, Stevie! They've left you!"

CHAPTER

THEY WEREN'T GONE. JESSE HADN'T THROWN UP. And Misha hadn't turned himself in to the police.

Yet.

The two of them were sitting in Old Pete. The car was running. So, I was glad to see, was the car heater.

"Shove over," I said, jamming into the wide front seat beside Jesse. We sat there for a while, staring straight ahead. Not much of a view – a garage with a snowmobile parked in front and, behind, a scrawny tree poking out of the snow. Wire fences disappeared into the dark in both directions.

"What did Veda Bickel say?" I asked Misha finally.

"Nothing."

Right. Nothing.

"Veda Bickel," muttered Jesse. "Rhymes with eat-a-pickle. I bet she ate one right before the meeting. What a sourpuss!"

Misha grunted.

Old Pete's engine made a gurgling noise, then coughed like an old man with a cold.

In a voice almost too low to hear, Misha said, "I'm going to do it. Turn myself in." Then he said a word I won't repeat and whacked the steering wheel with his open palm. "Nobody believes me, anyway. Might as well get it over with."

"Yeah, but – " said Jesse.

"Forget it." Misha slammed the car into gear. "I know you're trying to help, Jesse. But there's no point. They're going to nail me, no matter what I do."

I couldn't think of a thing to say. Neither could Jesse, I guess. We drove home in silence.

Bobbi was waiting up for us. She took one look at Misha and coaxed him into the living room for a private talk. Jesse and I hung out in the kitchen.

"Sorry," he said.

"For what?"

"For the lousy holiday. It's not exactly Happy New Year around here."

"It's not your fault."

"I know. I just wish there was some way we could prove that Misha's innocent."

So did I. But it was looking worse all the time. Suddenly a horrible thought occurred to me. What if Misha *wasn't* innocent? What if he had actually done it? The evidence – Old Pete spotted at the scene of the crime – was pretty strong. And tonight Misha had refused to go into the solarium. Why? And now he wanted to turn himself in.

"Jesse?"

"Uh, huh?"

"Are you *sure* Misha's innocent?"

"WHAATT???"

Quickly I listed my reasons for wondering. By the time I finished, Jesse's hands were fists, grinding into his cheeks as he hunched over the kitchen table. "He didn't do it, Stevie."

"Okay. So who did?"

Jesse's eyes searched Bobbi's kitchen, as if he expected the thief to pop out of the toaster or peek from behind the fridge. "What about Lester?" he said finally.

"Lester! Why Lester?"

"Didn't you see how bloodthirsty he was?" Jesse started pacing the kitchen. "Didn't you hear the way he talked about poor Joe Insect?"

"Yeah, well – " I didn't know how to tell Jesse that I'd sort of enjoyed it.

"I don't trust that guy, Stevie. There's something very weird about a guy who *enjoys* the death of insects!"

"Yeah, well ..." I said again. Actually, I kind of enjoy the death of certain insects myself. Mosquitoes, for instance. Flies. Wasps. Fleas.

Bobbi poked her head around the kitchen door. "Time for you two to get some sleep," she said, trying to smile.

I went to bed feeling rotten. I didn't *want* the thief to be Misha. But if there's one thing I've learned about detecting, it's this: you don't get to *pick* the person who did the crime.

I sure wished I could.

The next morning, Jesse was bleary-eyed. "I didn't sleep a wink," he moaned.

"Why not?"

He gave me a look. "Have you forgotten that I'm sharing a bedroom with a bunch of leafy savages? Insects are going to their death in that room, Stevie. All night long, I kept hearing their tiny insect screams ..."

"Insects don't scream, Jesse. Anyhow, it's the middle of winter. There *are* no insects. Those plants are probably on a diet."

Bobbi set orange juice down in front of us. "Well, you're half right, Stevie. The natural insects are dormant right now. But Misha *does* sometimes raise a few fruit flies to feed his plants."

"See?" said Jesse. "I knew it!"

"They don't scream, Jesse."

"How do *you* know?"

Misha was outside, shovelling the driveway. I guess Bobbi had talked him out of turning himself in because she said he was going to take us skating.

"Skating! But we were going to work on the case." I was thinking about those footprints in Muffy's yard. I wanted to get a closer look at them, in daylight.

Bobbi shook her head. "I'm worried about Misha. He needs to get his mind off things, enjoy himself a little – and he loves skating."

I thought it over as I ate breakfast. Maybe skating wasn't such a bad idea. It would give me a chance to question Misha. Something else occurred to me, too. Maybe some of the flirting techniques I'd been reading about could be useful in my detecting. There was one, for instance, called Establishing Rapport. As far as I could tell, Rapport was just a warm friendly feeling between two people. You made it happen by showing a Sincere Interest – asking about the other person's hobbies and stuff.

Okay, so skating was one of Misha's hobbies. If I were Sincerely Interested in skating, I could probably Establish a bunch of Rapport with him. Maybe I could get him to open up and tell me all the inside stuff he knew about the other club members. Skating slowly around an ice rink with Misha – perfect!

Half an hour later, bundled up like a sausage and carrying an ancient pair of skates that belonged to Bobbi, I trudged outside with the guys.

Misha surprised me by walking right past Old Pete. "We're going to Oliver's house," he said.

"Oliver is Misha's best friend," Jesse explained.

Misha led us across the road and down a driveway to a house where a guy and a little girl stood in the front window. Misha waved and pointed behind the house. The guy in the window nodded.

"We'll meet them out back," said Misha.

Out back? Misha and Jesse took a cleared path around the house. A moment later, I understood.

"*Here?*" I said. "In the backyard?"

Unbelievable. There was a huge open ice-skating rink right outside Oliver's back door. It had Christmas lights around it, hockey nets at either end and a bench on one side

"Oliver's dad floods the backyard every winter," Misha said as he pulled off his boots. "We spend half our lives out here."

Oliver – a tall, thin teenager – came outside with his skates on. He was followed by a girl who looked about eight – his sister, Mary Beth, we found out. Soon we were twirling in circles on the rink.

At least, *they* were twirling. It only took a minute to realize that everybody here was a really good skater. Except me. Oh, I can get from one end of the rink to the other without falling over. But if you only go skating three or four times a year, you're not exactly ready for the Olympics.

The rest of them *were* ready. Mary Beth was doing those things they do on TV – toe loops and axels and spins. Jesse, who took hockey lessons in Vancouver, could skate backwards faster than I skate forwards. And Misha and Oliver? Don't even ask.

"Loosen up, Stevie," called Jesse, as he whipped past me for the third time. "Glide! See? Glide!"

"Yeah, yeah," I said, lurching forward. "I'm gliding already."

Oliver disappeared and returned with a bunch of hockey sticks and a puck.

Uh, oh.

"I don't want to play," said Mary Beth. "I'm practising my routine."

"Well, practise down at the other end, okay?" Oliver handed a stick to Misha and one to Jesse. Then he looked at me. "How about you?"

I remembered Rapport. Grabbing a stick, I smiled. "Batter up," I said.

Steadying myself on the ice, I lowered the stick carefully into position. By the time I glanced up, all three guys were spinning around me in dizzying circles. The puck rocketed between them so fast I could hardly follow it with my eyes.

Oliver turned, shot – WHACK! – and the puck

flew between my feet.

He grinned at me. He had a handsome fox-type face with sharp features, and his teeth were dazzling white in the sunshine. "Are you sure you're up for this?"

I gave him a look. "Isn't there some position where you don't have to *skate* so much?"

Oliver grinned wider. "Sure! You can be goalie."

"Better put the full gear on her," said Misha. "We don't want her to get killed."

The next thing I knew I was being bundled into a whole new layer of clothes. A helmet-mask-thing I could barely see out of. Two huge padded pieces strapped to my legs. More heavy padding for my chest, back and arms. And the gloves! They looked like they were made for a gorilla.

"I can't move my fingers," I said.

"Don't worry about it!" Oliver propped me upright in front of the net and handed me an extra-fat hockey stick. I could barely get a grip on it.

"What do I do?"

"Easy," he said. "Just stop the puck!"

Right.

Just stop the puck.

Thirty seconds later, it sailed past my ear and hit the metal frame of the net with a PING! that nearly deafened me.

"The crowd goes WILD!" screamed Jesse, whipping past me in a haze of flying ice.

Whack! The puck flew past again, so fast I didn't even see it. It bounced off something metal-sounding and hit me in the backside, which was *not* padded.

"OWWW!"

"He shoots! He scores!" howled Oliver. He was behind me – no, in front of me – no, behind me. And the puck was – where was the –

Plop.

"Get up, Stevie. Goalies don't sit down."

"I know that. I fell!"

"Well, get up then."

I tried. What I discovered is, it's almost impossible to stand up when your knees won't bend.

"Get up, Stevie."

Whish! Whoosh! Whissssh! The guys flew past like bullets. Somehow I struggled to my feet.

I lasted another ten minutes. The goalie job, I decided, was stupid. You stand there in the freezing cold, wearing a totally ridiculous outfit, trying to stop a hard rubber object from smashing into your face at a hundred kilometres an hour.

Stupid.

Besides, I wasn't finding out a single thing about the case.

"I don't want to play anymore," I said. "I'm cold. My fingers are numb."

Oliver laughed as he whizzed by. I'm almost sure I heard him mutter, "Wimp!"

I shuffled over to the bench in a huff. Me? Stevie Diamond? A wimp? Hah!

Mary Beth joined me on the bench. "My hamster is lost."

"Uh huh," I grunted, struggling out of the goalie gear.

"It's not really my hamster. It's the school hamster. I brought it home for over Christmas. And now it's lost."

"Oh. Too bad."

"Misha said you guys are detectives. Do you find missing hamsters?"

I shook my head. "We already have a case. Anyhow, we don't do hamsters."

"Oh."

"Don't worry. Hamsters are like that. It'll turn up when it gets hungry enough."

Oliver's dad came outside just then with steaming hot chocolate. As we sipped, Mary Beth chattered to Jesse about her hamster. Fortunately, she seemed to have given up on the idea of hiring us as hamster detectives.

Jesse finished his hot chocolate and started racing around the rink again, whacking the puck back and forth. Mary Beth offered to show me a few figure-skating moves. I was experimenting with skating backwards when I overheard Oliver talking to Misha.

"Do you think I could borrow Old Pete tonight? I want to take Vanessa to the Sewer Rats concert, but my dad's using the car."

"Sure," said Misha. "The keys are in the glove compartment, like always."

Like always?

Keeping my back to Misha and Oliver, I edged closer to hear them better.

"The Sewer Rats!" Misha whistled. "Man, that must be costing you big bucks."

Oliver laughed. "It's okay. I'm feeling rich."

"No kidding," said Misha. "You must be – Stevie! What are you *doing?*"

Falling into his lap is what. I'd been listening so hard I hadn't noticed how close I was getting, and

I'd collapsed backwards – right across his legs. Using his cheek as a grip, I managed to pull myself up.

"Sorry."

From the look on his face, I could tell. This was *not* Rapport.

"Hey, Stevie, you skated backwards!" Mary Beth flew to a stop in front of me. "Halfway across the rink!"

I looked around. She was right. But no time to think about that now. Not when I had a brand new breakthrough in the stolen plants case. I skated as fast as I could – forwards, this time – over to Jesse.

He grinned at me. "Nice move, Stevie. When are you going to give Misha his cheek back?"

"Never mind that. I have to talk to you. Alone."

It wasn't easy convincing him to leave, especially when Oliver invited us inside. I had to wiggle my eyebrows, jerk my head and even wink to get the message across.

"What's going on?" Jesse asked as we walked down the driveway.

"We have a whole new suspect."

Jesse stopped in his tracks. "Who?"

"Oliver."

"Oliver! He's not even in the club."

"I know, but listen. Oliver drives Old Pete! Misha leaves the keys in the glove compartment, and Oliver can just borrow the car any time he feels like it."

"You mean it could have been *Oliver* driving Old Pete on the night of the theft?"

"Exactly! Misha was listening to music, remember? He wouldn't even have heard the car drive away."

Jesse bit his lip with excitement. "Stevie, this is incredible."

"That's not all." I stomped my feet to keep warm. "Oliver's taking his girlfriend to an expensive rock concert tonight. He said he felt rich."

Jesse's eyes bulged. "From selling the plants?"

I shrugged. "It fits, doesn't it?"

Jesse held up a mittened hand. "Wait a minute, Stevie. Oliver's not in the Carnivore Club. How would he get the inside information – like about Muffy taking a sleeping pill?"

I thought for a second.

"From Misha!" I said. "They're best buddies, right? And neighbours? Just like us." Whenever Jesse and I did interesting stuff, we always told each other all about it.

"Stevie, you're right. It has to be him. Do you think he brought the stolen plants back to his house? Do you – oh, my gosh!" Jesse staggered to a stop.

"What?"

"Mary Beth's hamster!" he gasped.

"The hamster? What about – " Suddenly I got it. "Oh, my gosh."

"I can't believe it," whispered Jesse. "Poor Sigmund."

"Sigmund?"

"That's his name. The hamster."

I shook my head. "That *was* his name."

Closing his eyes, Jesse nodded slowly. "One of those vicious vegetables *ate* poor Sigmund!"

CHAPTER

"I WISH WE COULD MAKE A CITIZEN'S ARREST," I SAID. "Go right back there this second and and nab Oliver."

"I wish we could arrest those plants!" Jesse was practically spitting with anger.

"Oh, right! We could lock them up in little plant handcuffs. Stick them in jail, throw away the key."

"Don't make jokes, Stevie. When I think of poor little Sigmund – " Jesse took a deep breath, trying to get a grip on his emotions. "What are we going to do?"

"We have to go back. We have to search Oliver's house from top to bottom."

"Yeah!" said Jesse. "We have to – wait a minute! We can't just go busting in there and start searching. What'll we tell Oliver? And Misha?"

"Easy!" I headed back towards Oliver's. "Mary Beth tried to hire me this morning. She practically begged me to look for Sigmund."

"So?"

"So we'll take the case," I said. "Everyone will *think* we're looking for Sigmund. Really we'll be looking for evidence against Oliver."

When Mary Beth came to the door, we told her we'd decided to take the hamster case after all. She gave us a huge smile and thanked us about ten times each. Jesse and I exchanged guilty looks. Poor Mary Beth. Chances were good she was never going to see that hamster alive again.

Oliver and Misha were fooling around with the computer in the basement, so we started our search on the main floor. Cupboards, closets, under and behind furniture – the usual. It took almost half an hour to go over all the rooms. When Mary Beth's dad found out what we were doing, he thanked us, too, and offered us doughnuts. I felt guiltier than ever.

Mary Beth charged downstairs ahead of us to tell Oliver and Misha we were coming.

"Hamster detecting?" asked Misha. "Whose idea was this?"

Mary Beth looked at Jesse, who pointed at me.

Misha shook his head and turned back to the computer.

The computer was in a rec room, which also had some couches and a TV. We checked it out quickly and then searched a laundry room and a room with a huge furnace. Finally, the only thing left was a closed door next to the computer. I turned the doorknob.

"Hey!" Oliver leaped to his feet. "That's my bedroom! What do you think you're doing?"

"Looking for Sigmund."

"That's private!"

I peered into the dark room. In the far corner, I thought I could see the outline of –

Oliver slammed the door in my face.

Plants!

"But Sigmund – "

"Forget it! Go detect somewhere else. There are *no* runaway rodents in my bedroom."

He was half a foot taller than me and ten times as mad. I backed off. Jesse and I made a show of searching the rec room one last time, but of course we didn't find anything. When we left, Mary Beth looked close to tears. I guess I hadn't realized how much she'd counted on us.

"Maybe he'll still turn up," I said.

"Sure," muttered Jesse. "He'll probably, er, turn up."

But all I could think of as we walked home was … Sigmund soup.

"There were plants in Oliver's room, Jesse."

"Carnivorous plants?"

"I don't know. I didn't get a good enough look. Oliver nearly took my fingers off, slamming that door."

Jesse nodded. "He's definitely hiding something."

Turning into Bobbi's driveway, we spotted the line of cars.

"Oh, geez." Jesse smacked his head. "The relatives. I forgot they were coming."

"The relatives?"

"Yeah! I've got a million of them. Aunts, uncles, cousins, second cousins, great-aunts – the works. No more detecting today."

"But, Jesse, the case is hot. Can't we just ignore your dumb relatives and – "

"Ignore *my* relatives?" He sighed. "Not a chance!"

He was right. They were the kissy-huggy-talky kind of relatives, and they swooped us up into a noisy visit that lasted for hours. The first few minutes were awful – getting hugged by thirty strangers is not my idea of a good time. After that, it got better. The best part was the food. Bobbi had cooked up a ton of Ukrainian food – tiny cabbage rolls filled with bacon and rice called *holupchi*, garlic-and-ham sausage called *kobasa,* and those yummy little dumplings full of potato and cheese called *perogies*. What you do, I discovered, is plaster loads of sour cream over the whole works. It kind of finishes things off. Then there were the desserts – date squares, blueberry pie and my old favourite, lemon meringue tarts.

"I'm stuffed," I moaned to Jesse after my third tart. "This relative thing is great!"

"Easy for you," he said glumly. "They're not hauling out *your* baby pictures."

A bunch of Jesse's aunts and uncles were crouched over some old photo albums. I'd been careful not to get too close. If there's one thing in the world that's *not* interesting, it's other people's baby pictures. Jesse's relatives, though, thought they were wonderful.

"Look! There he is in his jolly bouncer. Uncle Bob didn't read the directions, and he put it together wrong, remember? Poor little Jesse took two jumps and flipped right over!"

"That's right! He bounced four times upside-down before we could get to him!"

Giggle, giggle. "Awww … poor little precious."

"Oh, look! Here's where he went through that chubby stage. Gosh, look at his legs. Remember what we used to call him?"

Shrieks of laughter. "Thunder Thighs!"

"Hardy, har, har," muttered Jesse.

"Here he is with no clothes on. Oh, isn't he sweet …"

Jesse groaned and stuffed his head under a pillow.

With Jesse and me, the relatives were noisy and excited. But around Misha, they were different – quiet and careful. I guess they must have heard about the theft. One by one, they went over to talk to him – give him a pat on the shoulder or just sit with him for a while. Misha didn't say much. Just nodded and chewed his lip a lot.

Finally, after a lot more noise and hugs, the relatives left. Bobbi was shocked at how late it was and hurried Jesse and me off to bed, but we managed a last whispered conference in the hall.

"Got a plan for tomorrow?" asked Jesse.

I nodded. "Oliver's house. Somehow or other, we have *got* to get inside that room."

CHAPTER

8

AT BREAKFAST THE NEXT DAY, AFTER A QUICK GLANCE at me, Jesse asked Misha if he would take us skating again. "At Oliver's house. It was so much fun yesterday."

But Misha shook his head. "I'm driving over to the Conservatory today. The people who run it were really disappointed that we had to cancel the carnivore exhibition. I thought I'd take a few of my plants over so they'd have *something* to show visitors."

"What a good idea," said Bobbi. "You can take Stevie and Jesse with you. I'm sure they'd find the Conservatory interesting."

Misha shook his head. "I already invited Oliver."

Bobbi's voice was firm. "There's room for Stevie and Jesse, too." And that was that.

Oh, well. Maybe when we picked Oliver up, I could still make up an excuse to go inside – and sneak into that bedroom! Jesse and I bundled up quickly and headed for the door.

"Wait here," said Misha. "I have to warm up Old Pete."

Oh. Good idea.

I watched through the window as he scraped snow and ice off the windshield. Clouds of grey exhaust rose from the rear. Misha pulled a cord out of what looked like a plug at the front of the car.

"What's that?" I asked Jesse.

"An electric cord. In the winter here, you plug your car in when it's parked so the motor doesn't freeze."

"You mean, all over the city, cars are plugged in – like toasters?"

Jesse nodded. "Yup."

I was still thinking this over when I spotted Oliver walking down our driveway. Rats! So much for sneaking into his room.

We all piled into Old Pete.

"Here!" Misha dumped a plastic-covered plant onto my lap. He handed one to Oliver, too, and brought a third for Jesse. Taking one look at Jesse's face, I reached for the plant. "I'll hold that."

Jesse smiled weakly. "Thanks."

We drove past farm fields that were dazzling bright and dotted with cross-country skiers. When we reached the city, we could see clouds rising everywhere – exhaust from cars and trucks, and breath from people's mouths. Oliver got into a tour-guide mood and started pointing things out to me and Jesse – the Red River, the museum, the concert hall, the theatre centre.

"And here's our famous intersection, Portage and Main."

"Why is it famous?" I asked.

"Coldest spot in the city – where Portage Avenue

meets Main Street. See how wide those streets are? When it's windy and the cold whips through here, it zaps you from every direction at once. Man, it's fierce!"

Misha shivered. "My mom told me that in the old days the police directing traffic on this corner used to wear long buffalo-skin coats."

I glanced at the street sign. Looked pretty ordinary to me. But one thing I had learned about Winnipeg is that you can't tell much about the *outside* when you're looking at it from the *inside*.

Finally, we reached the Conservatory. Before he went to park, Misha dropped us off at the front door so we could run in with the plants. The Conservatory was an enormous brick building roofed in glass and filled with green plants, most of them large and unusual-looking.

As we walked towards the front desk, Oliver stumbled and stepped on my heel. I was about to tell him to watch it when I remembered.

The Accidental Encounter. I'd read about it in *Super Teen*. It was a flirting technique! If you wanted somebody to notice you, you just accidentally-on-purpose bumped into them.

Was it possible? Could Oliver be flirting with *me*?

Well, why not? He *was* a teenager. And he'd been pretty friendly in the car.

I thought hard. Maybe this could be useful. Detective useful, I mean. Maybe, if I flirted back, I could get the truth out of him. There was this flirting technique that was in all the magazines that I hadn't even tried yet. The Romantic Sniff. Pretty simple, really. You just tell the other person how good they smell. I know, it sounds dumb. But it was right there in the magazines.

Leaning towards Oliver, I sniffed delicately. "Mmmm. Something sure smells good around here."

Oliver sniffed, too. He glanced around. "French fries," he said. "Tell Misha I'll be in the cafeteria."

I watched him disappear down the hall.

Great.

I shrugged and joined Jesse, who was talking to the woman behind the front desk. She thanked us for bringing in the plants and invited us to look around, so we did a little wander through the Conservatory. It had some great banana plants, with green bananas as big as sausages on them. Also some miniature orange trees and loads of enormous jungle-type vines. A pond in the middle had tropical fish and a wishing well. Tossing in a penny, I made a wish – that I could get a better handle on this flirting thing. Was there some special trick to it? Something I was missing?

We found Misha back at the front desk, talking to the Conservatory woman.

"It's a real shame," she was saying as we walked up. "The exhibit would have been very popular. A lot of children phoned to ask about it. We were hoping it would be the beginning of something much larger – a whole new wing of the Conservatory dedicated to carnivorous plants."

"A whole wing?" repeated Jesse.

She nodded. "There aren't many places where the public can go to see this kind of plant. They're very unusual."

"And this theft means there won't be a carnivore wing?" I asked.

She shrugged. "If we'd had the exhibit and it had been popular, I think a carnivore wing would have been a sure thing. Now I'm not so sure. Other garden clubs have been putting on the pressure – the Prairie Plants Club, for example. And the Cactus Lovers – they'd like a wing of desert plants. And, of course, the Orchid Society. Mrs. Flaversham, their president, has been rather insistent that it be an orchid wing."

"What's insistent?" Jesse whispered in my ear.

"Pushy," I whispered back.

"She sounds like a pain," he muttered. "Like Veda Bickel. Maybe *all* garden club presidents are creeps."

I nodded. Remembering Veda's huge spidery eyes and how they had fastened on Misha at the meeting, I was glad it wasn't me she was picking on.

Misha, meanwhile, was shaking hands with the Conservatory woman. After thanking us again for bringing the plants, she disappeared into her office.

We found Oliver in the cafeteria, slouched on a plastic chair with his feet up on a second chair. He was polishing off an order of fries and gravy that looked good enough to stick around for, but Misha seemed to be in a hurry. We were almost out the door when Jesse stopped.

"Wait a sec."

Backing up a few steps, he peered at an opened newspaper held upright by two male hands. Then he peeked over the top. "Hey, it's Lester Potts. Hi, Lester!"

The newspaper came down a few centimetres to reveal Lester's pink face and startled eyes. "Goodness, what a surprise," he said.

We hello-ed and hi-ed a bit. Misha explained about bringing his plants in. "What are *you* doing here, Lester?" he asked.

The newspaper dropped a few centimetres more. "Well, I ... uh ... often come here, you know, just to roam around. Such a lovely, peaceful spot. All these plants."

Jesse looked puzzled. "But Misha told us you own a flower shop."

"Oh, I do, I do. But one can never get enough of green, living things, can one?"

I was about to ask Lester whether he was going to eat *all* his fries when I noticed a woman staring at us from the doorway. She was a mousy-looking woman with a pinchy little nose, and she was wearing a drab brown coat.

I nudged Jesse, but he ignored me. "Do you sell carnivorous plants in your flower shop, Lester?" he asked.

The woman was still staring. No, glaring. At us? But why?

"Oh, no," Lester was saying. "I'd love to carry carnivores, but, well . . . it's a very ordinary sort of shop, I'm afraid. Perhaps it's *too* ordinary. Business has been a little slow lately, and – oh dear!"

The newspaper was up again, blocking his face entirely.

Misha blinked. "Well, uh, I guess we'll be going."

Lester's baby finger curled out from the newspaper in a little goodbye wave.

The mousy woman was pushing her way through the cafeteria lineup as we left. I touched Misha's elbow and pointed. "Do you know that woman? The one in the brown coat?"

He shook his head. "Never seen her before."

I stopped, confused. Some *very* strange things had just happened. Why was Lester holding his newspaper up that way? It was almost as if he were trying to hide from us. But why? And who was that strange woman? And why was she glaring at us?

My mind churned with these questions all the way home. It wasn't until we pulled into Oliver's driveway that I remembered – Jesse and I were supposed to search Oliver's room.

This was it. Our chance.

"Can we go inside for a minute?" I asked. "I think I … left something at Oliver's house yesterday."

"What?" asked Misha.

I thought fast. "Oh, uh, my sock!"

"Your sock?" Jesse frowned. "Stevie, you were *wearing* your socks when you went home yesterday. Both of them. I remember. They were blue with white stripes."

Thank you very much, Jesse Kulniki, I muttered to myself. Aloud, I said, "I know. But I also keep a sock in … in my pocket. For luck! It's my lucky sock."

Misha stared. "You have a lucky *sock?*"

I smiled brightly. "Doesn't everyone?"

It certainly didn't Establish any Rapport, but at least it got us into the house.

"What colour is your lucky sock?" asked Jesse as we stepped inside.

"I don't *have* a lucky sock!" I hissed in his ear. "I'm trying to get a look in Oliver's room!"

"Oh. Oh, right." Then louder, "I think I'll just, um, look for Stevie's lucky sock downstairs."

Which left the *upstairs* for me. So there I was – searching for a sock that didn't exist in the same places I had already searched for a hamster that didn't exist. I was peering under the couch when I heard Jesse's voice behind me.

"I did it!" he whispered. "I got into Oliver's room."

I turned. "Great! Did you find any plants?"

"Nope. But I did find this." He grinned and held out his hand. Cupped in his palm was a small pile of black dirt. I held out my hand, and he dumped the dirt into it. It felt damp and soft like the kind of dirt you grow plants in.

"It was on the floor," said Jesse, "in the far corner."

I sucked in my breath. "That's exactly where I saw the plants yesterday. Do you know what this means?"

He nodded. "Oliver must have gotten scared when you tried to look in there yesterday, Stevie. He *moved* the plants out."

We were so stunned by this thought that we didn't notice Misha and Oliver coming up behind us.

"Hey, guys!" said Misha.

Jesse and I whirled around, clunking heads. The dirt in my hand flew up in the air and rained down like a black shower.

All over Oliver.

CHAPTER

"WHAT THE – PPAAH!" SWATTING AT HIS EYES AND hair, Oliver spat dirt out of his mouth. "Ppuh! Pehhh!"

Misha's green eyes bulged behind his glasses as he turned to me. "*What* are you doing?"

"It was an accident!" I started brushing dirt off Oliver's shirt and hair. It scattered, making speckled patches on the white rug. Oliver spat out more pah's and peh's, along with a few extremely rude swear words.

"Should I, er, get the vacuum cleaner?" asked Jesse.

Misha glared at him. "I'm not even going to *ask* what your friend here was doing with a handful of dirt."

"She, uh – "

"Don't tell me. It was her lucky dirt, right?"

Jesse edged towards the door. "I'll get the vacuum cleaner."

Okay. So it wasn't the most professional detective work in the world. So we had to apologize, a lot, as we cleaned up the carpet. Still, as I told Jesse, once we were back alone in Bobbi's laundry room, we were making progress. The evidence against Oliver was getting stronger. Maybe it was time to let Misha in on our suspicions.

"Are you kidding?" Jesse nearly lost his perch on top of the washing machine. "Oliver is his best friend in the world. Misha's never going to believe Oliver stole those plants."

Hmmm. Jesse was right. Those two were tighter than sardines in a can. It was going to take more than a handful of dirt to convince Misha his best friend had set him up.

Besides, even if Oliver was our *prime* suspect, was he our *only* suspect? True, the clues we'd discovered all pointed straight at him. But there were funny things going on with other people, too – things a detective just couldn't ignore.

Maybe it would help to write it all down.

Reaching into my jeans pocket, I pulled out a crumpled piece of paper. The name of my school was written at the top, followed by the words "Important Notice to Parents." It was dated early December.

Oh.

Well, it couldn't have been *that* important.

Flipping it over, I turned to Jesse. "Got a pen?"

A minute later we had the beginnings of a suspect list. It looked like this:

LIST OF SUSPECTS

1. OLIVER – PLANTS AND DIRT IN ROOM
   – MISSING HAMSTER
   – BORROWS OLD PETE
   – SAYS HE FEELS RICH

"Boy," said Jesse. "That's a lot of evidence against Oliver."

I nodded. "Looks bad all right. Okay, who else?"

"Eat-a-Pickle," said Jesse. "Write her name down."

"You mean Veda Bickel?"

Jesse nodded. "You heard her at that meeting. She hates Misha, and she's out to get him."

I wrote Veda's name under Oliver's.

"There," I said. "Now what about Lester Potts? Did you notice how he acted today? Like he had something to hide?"

Jesse nodded. "I never trusted that guy for a second. Remember the way he talked about poor Joe Insect? It was – "

I cut him off by telling him about the mousy-looking woman who'd glared at us in the Conservatory cafeteria.

"Are you sure she was glaring, Stevie? Maybe she was just looking in our general direction."

"She was glaring, Jesse. She was even peering around other people so she could keep her eye on us."

"A member of the Carnivore Club maybe?"

I shook my head. "Misha didn't recognize her."

We argued a bit about whether we should add her to our list. Jesse said he didn't want any people we didn't know on the list.

"It's not a party, Jesse. We don't have to know her personally."

In the end, we compromised by putting her at the bottom under the heading "Questions." The final list looked like this:

LIST OF SUSPECTS

1. OLIVER — PLANTS AND DIRT IN ROOM
   — MISSING HAMSTER
   — BORROWS OLD PETE
   — SAYS HE FEELS RICH
2. VEDA BICKEL — HATES MISHA
   — OUT TO GET HIM?
3. LESTER POTTS — ACTED WEIRD AT CONSERVATORY
   — ENJOYS THE DEATH OF INSECTS

QUESTION:
WHO IS THE MOUSY-LOOKING WOMAN IN BROWN???

I stared hard at the list. Then I sighed. Every single name had a problem. For instance, Oliver looked guilty – but did he really know enough about carnivorous plants to steal only the most valuable ones? Veda and Lester were both plant experts – but they didn't drive Old Pete.

Was it possible that there was more than one thief? Two thieves working together?

"I'm more confused than ever," said Jesse.

I nodded. "Me, too. What we need is a plan. Some way to get the thief – or thieves – out into the open."

"Right," said Jesse, squinting. "A plan."

He scrunched up into thinking position, while I paced beside a pile of dirty laundry. There's something about walking, I've discovered, that gets your brain going – some weird connection between your head and feet. Pretty soon my mind was racing along at computer-speed.

Then it happened. Pieces of a plan started snapping into place like blocks of Lego. Not just any plan, either – an absolutely brilliant plan! But could we pull it off? Here was the hard part – we'd need Misha's help.

"What is it, Stevie? You look funny."

"Jesse, I've got it! What we have to do to catch the plant thief is *use the methods of the plants themselves.*"

"What??"

"The carnivorous plants! You know how they trap insects? Well, that's how you and I are going to trap the thief."

He looked confused. "We're going to lure the thief with our nectar?"

"In a way," I said. "What does the thief want?"

He shrugged. "Valuable carnivorous plants to sell for tons of money."

"Exactly! That's the nectar – the bait. We lure the thief with new and even *more* valuable carnivorous plants into Bobbi's greenhouse. But it's a trap! When the thief shows up to steal the plants, we're waiting. We can even make a sticky trap like those plants have – gooey stuff his feet will get stuck in."

"Right!" Jesse's eyes were eager. "First we lure him with – wait a minute, Stevie! Where are we going to get a bunch of valuable carnivorous plants?"

"We don't have to! There won't really *be* any carnivorous plants in the greenhouse, Jesse. We just have to make the thief *think* they're here. We'll get Misha to tell everyone in the club that he's received a delivery of valuable new plants."

"What about Oliver?"

"That'll be tricky," I agreed. "We want Oliver to hear about the new plants, but we don't want him to know that it's a trap." I gnawed on a knuckle.

"Don't worry, I'll figure out something. In the meantime, we'd better get Misha."

"Uh, Stevie?" Jesse hopped down from the washer. "Maybe I'd better talk to Misha alone."

"Why?" I tried to slip past, but he blocked the doorway.

"Well, uh, I don't know how to say this, but – "

"But what?"

"Misha thinks you're a – a little strange."

"What?"

"Well, that's not exactly what he said, but – "

"What *did* he say?"

"Well, nothing really. I just – "

"Jesse, for heaven's sake, I'm not a baby. Spit it out!"

"You really want to know?"

"YES!"

"Okay, he called you a dingbat."

"A dingbat?"

"A dingbat. Also a nut-case and a ditzy, pea-brained looney tune. He said you were – do you want his exact words? – a few pickles short of a full jar."

For a second, Jesse looked pleased with himself. He even giggled. Then something – probably the expression on my face – made his forehead wrinkle in alarm.

"Ditzy?" I repeated.

"Now, Stevie, he – "

"Pea-brained?"

"Well, yeah, but I think – "

"I don't believe this."

"Wait a minute, I – "

"I don't BELEEEVE this!"

Jesse's voice was quick and nervous. "Now, Stevie, look at it from Misha's point of view. You *have* been doing some pretty strange things. Like those clothes you showed up in at the airport? And falling in his lap at the skating rink? Not to mention the lucky sock – and the dirt in Oliver's face."

"Jesse Kulniki, that was *your* dirt!"

"Well, yeah, but you threw it."

There was nothing else to say.

Nothing.

Pushing past him, I ran to my room and slammed the door so hard the walls shook. Good! I hoped a heavy picture would fall down – right on Misha's head. I hoped his stupid plants would shrivel up and die. I hoped his stupid car would catch on fire. I hoped a hundred police would come and drag him by his stupid feet to jail.

Pea brain.

It was so unfair.

I decided to stay in my room for the rest of the time we were in Winnipeg.

"Stevie? Are you hungry?" Bobbi peeked around the door, a lemon tart in her hand. When she spotted me huddled on the bed, her eyes widened with concern. "Is anything wrong?"

What a nice grandma. Like out of a storybook. How could I tell her that her youngest son – already accused of being a criminal – was also a heartless crumb?

I took the tart. "Nothing's wrong."

"Well, good, because it's time to get dressed and go over to Fern's and Bob's. Have you forgotten that it's New Year's Eve?"

I had, totally.

The last thing I felt like doing was partying with Jesse's relatives, but there was no choice. One thing, though, I was *not* going to dress up. I threw on my oldest jeans and my most comfortable sweatshirt, the one with the grape-juice stain across the front.

Nobody noticed. Nobody cared. Misha didn't even glance my way. Jesse just grinned stupidly, happy to see me.

For the rest of the evening, I spoke as little as humanly possible. We played board games and charades at Uncle Bob's and Aunt Fern's house and ate a table-full of sausage rolls, deep-fried shrimp, tiny pizza-buns and quiche. At midnight we watched New Year's at Times Square on TV and counted down the numbers – ten, nine, eight …

That's where I cut out. No way I was hugging and kissing that rat, Misha. Or that junior rat, Jesse. I hid in the bathroom while everyone sang that dumb New Year's song about old acquaintance being forgot. Hah! My old acquaintance around here was Jesse, and I couldn't wait to forget *him*.

New Year's Day was more of the same. More Kulniki relatives, more food, more party. I sat by myself in a corner of Aunt Lulu's living room, reading an old magazine.

"Hey, Stevie?"

It was the junior rat.

"I'm busy."

Jesse looked at my magazine. "Since when do you read *Hockey Life?*"

I gave him a withering stare.

He grinned back. Jesse is a very hard guy to wither.

"Listen, Stevie, I think I talked Misha into going along with our plan. It wasn't easy. At first, he thought it was sort of dumb. So I asked if he had any better ideas, and of course he didn't. Then I reminded him of all the other cases I – er, we – had solved. I pointed out that even if it doesn't work, so what? No harm done, right? Finally, he agreed. He's going to do it, Stevie. He's going to try our plan!"

"*Our* plan?"

"Hey, don't be like that. Who cares whose plan as long as it works? Will you do it? Will you help?"

"I'll think about it. *After* I finish my magazine."

He wandered off, and I sat there for five minutes more, turning the pages of *Hockey Life* and listening to the voices arguing in my brain.

Voice One: Why should you help Misha? He called you a pea brain.

Voice Two: Yeah, but it's such a great plan. If you say no, you won't be part of it, and you won't get any credit for thinking it up.

Voice One: Hah! You won't get any credit, anyway.

Voice Two: Who cares? Do you want to spend the rest of your holiday reading *Hockey Life?*

Voice One didn't have a chance. No way I could sit back and let those Kulniki guys take over *my* plan. I found Jesse over by the food table, eating the last piece of stuffed celery.

"Okay," I said, "here's what we're going to do ..."

It was even easier than I'd hoped. Misha only had to phone one person – Muffy, the club's phoning secretary. Jesse and I listened on an extension. I have to admit that Misha did a great job. He described the plants as if they really existed. He told Muffy that he'd ordered them through his mother's greenhouse business and hadn't expected them to be delivered so soon. He said he thought the plants might even make the exhibit possible again.

Muffy went into her usual flap. "Oh my – oh yes – well, certainly I'll call the other members to tell them. They'll be so – oh goodness me – "

She must have gotten right on the job. Within an hour, both Veda Bickel and Lester Potts had called. Lester wanted to hear about the plants in detail – what kind, how big and all that. Veda flipped out totally. She called Misha a grubby little under-aged upstart and accused him of trying to take over the club. He wouldn't get away with it, she yelled, not as long as *she* was president. Finally, she hung up in his ear.

The problem of how to tell Oliver solved itself. He phoned while Misha was in the shower.

"What do I do?" hissed Jesse, his hand over the receiver.

"Tell him Misha's not here," I whispered back. "Tell him Misha went to pick up a new shipment of valuable carnivorous plants."

He did. Oliver bought it. So far, so good.

We were a little bit worried about Bobbi. True, she *had* asked us to help. But I wasn't sure how she'd feel about a sticky, gooey mess on her greenhouse floor. As Jesse went off to tell her, I reminded him to say that it would be a very *tidy* sort of mess.

"She's in her room," he said when he returned, "with one of her migraine headaches. I couldn't tell her, Stevie. She was groaning."

I nodded. Now it was just me, Misha, Jesse and –

The trap.

CHAPTER

TAKE IT FROM ME – AT TWO O'CLOCK IN THE morning, a greenhouse can be a *very* spooky place. Dead quiet, for one thing, except for strange whooshes from the furnace and sudden flutters among the leaves. Dark, too, with shadows that seem to be waiting, like black holes, for a chance to suck you in. And damp – the kind that settles on your skin like a wet cloth and stays there. After a while you can't help feeling that things are *growing* in your direction – hundreds of scrawny tendrils, crawling, reaching out like skinny little arms ...

I was glad there weren't *really* any carnivorous plants in there.

Jesse and I were sitting in the dark, crouched underneath a small wooden table.

Waiting.

We'd been waiting for three hours.

In my right hand was a flashlight. In my left was a walkie-talkie. The other half of the walkie-talkie set was with Misha in the living room of the house.

We had every move planned. If the thief showed up, Jesse and I would immediately whisper the news over the walkie-talkie to Misha. Misha would immediately phone the police. The police would immediately come and arrest the thief, who would be stuck like a bug to the brilliant trap Jesse and I had made.

If I squinted hard, I could almost see it – a dark pool on the concrete floor, a couple of metres away. We had gone through all of Bobbi's cupboards and closets, pulling out everything that was sticky. Honey. Glue. Molasses. Rubber cement. Corn syrup. Floor-tile adhesive. Roofing tar.

Just inside the greenhouse door, we'd started pouring. The goo had spread, swirling into different colours and patterns, like car oil on a puddle. The edges were kind of sloppy, and the pool was a bit bigger than we'd planned. Okay, a lot bigger. But it stuck great. Jesse and I touched just a tiny bit and, after washing our fingers for ten minutes, we still couldn't get the sticky orange stain off.

Misha had showed up just as we finished. He'd taken one look and laughed. A friendly kind of laugh – I think. He said it was a not-bad imitation of a sundew. But would it really hold a human being? Jesse and I showed him our fingers, but he still looked doubtful. I don't know what he expected. The only way to test it would be for someone to jump in, and I didn't hear *him* volunteering.

We'd argued for almost half an hour about who would hide in the greenhouse and who would stay in the house. Misha insisted that he should be in the greenhouse because he was older and – get this – a guy. I said I should be in the greenhouse because it was my idea in the first place. When Misha heard *that*, he looked ready to back out of the whole thing, but, of course, it was too late. Jesse offered to stay in the house alone, but that would have put me and Misha in the greenhouse together, and we were still a long way from Rapport. In the end, Misha agreed to stay in the house by himself. The plan wouldn't work anyway, he said, so he might as well be comfortable.

Comfortable was exactly what Jesse and I were *not*. I was starting to wonder why I'd argued so hard to be in the greenhouse. The concrete floor was hard, damp and chilly on the backside. I squirmed, trying to find a better spot. Holding up a hand, I could barely make out my fingers.

"Jesse? You awake?"

No answer.

Rats. Asleep again.

"Jesse, wake up!"

"Hunh!?" A few snorts and gasps from my left. "What's happening?"

"Nothing. Keep your eyes open."

Silence. Then, "Stevie, I haven't had any sleep for days. Those plants in Misha's room have wiped me out. Can't we take turns watching? I'll do the second half of the night."

How could I admit I was scared to stay awake alone? I could just hear Misha: "I told you it should be *guys* in the greenhouse."

"Okay," I said. "I'll wake you up at three. But if I need you, you be ready!"

He mumbled something. Then I heard a soft snore. I was on my own.

Bobbi's house and greenhouse were out in the middle of flat fields on a small country road that led to her house and Oliver's house and four or five others. Not many cars came down it, and when they did, you could see the lights from a long way off. I knew that as long as we stayed awake, it would be hard for a car to get close without us spotting it.

If it was Oliver, of course, he would come on foot, but our hiding spot faced the door. All I had to do was stay alert …

I didn't fall asleep – I'm absolutely *sure* of that. But maybe I did get a little dozy. The problem was my chin, which kept ending up on my chest. Every time it happened, I sat up straight, blinking my eyes hard and opening them as wide as I could. Gradually, though, my eyelids would get heavier and …

I jerked upright at the sound of a distant motor. Not a car – it was too high-pitched. After a second, I remembered when I'd heard that sound before.

Summer days in Vancouver. A lawn mower?

Okay, maybe if I'd been more awake I would have wondered what a lawn mower was doing in the middle of a prairie winter. But I wasn't, so I didn't. Shining the flashlight on my watch, I saw that it was almost time for Jesse to wake up. In fifteen minutes, I could let *him* figure it out. In the meantime, maybe I could let my eyelids relax … just a little.

When I opened my eyes, something was … different. Have you ever had the feeling that someone's watching you? Someone you can't see? I tried to swallow, but my mouth was too dry. I caught my breath, and it seemed that even my heart stopped while I listened.

Whoosh.

Hiss.

Okay. Whoosh – that was the furnace. Hiss – that was the sprinklers. I let out a breath, then sucked it in again as I heard a snuffling sound. Just to my left! Every muscle in my body went stiff.

The snuffle got louder. It changed to a wheeze. Then finally, a snore.

Jesse.

I sighed. Nothing like a few hours in the dark to make your imagination go nuts. Relax, Stevie, I told myself. Remember, you're a detective. Detectives have nerves of steel. I peered at the door. Still shut. I squinted at the pool of goo. Still right where it was supposed to be. I listened again. Nothing but whooshes and hisses. I took a deep breath, then another.

Better.

Maybe I'd just been sitting still too long. I stretched both arms out straight. When my left hand touched wool, I jerked it back. Then I realized – just Jesse's sweater.

Boy, I really *was* spooked.

I stretched again. My right hand touched –

A face!

CHAPTER

"AAAIIIIIIEEEEEEEE!"

It took a few seconds to realize where the sound was coming from. Me! Panicky, screeching, I was scrambling across the floor on my hands and knees. Whonk! I lurched headfirst into a table leg. Warm air whooshed into my ear. Something hard and plastic under my right knee – ouch! – the walkie talkie. I punched at the buttons in the dark.

"HELP!" I yelled.

CRASH! Something hit the floor.

"AAAAEEEEEIII!" Another scream. Not me this time.

A thud, followed by an oof! A yelp, then a bang, then another thud.

I must have hit the receive-button on the walkie-talkie. I heard Misha. "What's happening? Are you guys – "

Did I hit another button? He was gone. The flashlight – where was it? My hand felt around on the concrete floor, swishing through a puddle of water, grabbing hold of a table leg. I smacked at all the buttons on the walkie-talkie again. "HELP! MISHA! POLICE!"

More crashes. Another yell. A voice in the dark. "Steeeveee?"

Suddenly the lights went on – so bright I had to cover my eyes. I heard a gasp and looked up. Misha and Bobbi were standing in the greenhouse doorway. Bobbi was wearing a red down jacket over blue flannel pyjamas. Her eyes bugged out as she stared at the floor in front of her.

The good news was – the trap had worked.

The bad news was – it had caught the wrong person.

Stuck in the pool of goo, like a fly caught in a sundew, was Jesse. He was sprawled on his backside with his hands, feet, legs and rear end caught in the mess. Somehow the stuff had gotten onto his hair and face, too, leaving thick, gross-looking orange smears across his cheeks and head. He tried to lift his right hand. It rose a few centimetres, strands of gunk still joining it to the pool, and then dropped back down to the floor. He gazed around, blinking.

Misha spoke first. "Jesse! What happened?"

Jesse shook his head, dazed. "I was in ... in Madison Square Garden, playing hockey against the New York Rangers. I was just about to score the winning goal when the fire alarm went off, right in my ear."

"That was me screaming," I said. "You were

asleep, Jesse."

He looked more confused than ever. "Anyway, I raced off the ice and – " He blinked at the pool of goo and shrugged.

Bobbi opened her mouth, then closed it when she heard the siren. We all turned to watch the headlights of the police car as it raced down the little country road and into our driveway. Seconds later, two police officers charged through the door, nearly knocking Bobbi off her feet. They got her straight again and apologized. Then they noticed Misha.

"You!" said the one with the glasses.

Things went downhill from there. When the police asked who had phoned, Misha had to admit it was him. He started to explain, but even to me it sounded like some stupid prank. Seems it's more or less against the law to call the police for fun, and that's what the officers thought Misha had done. They asked if he didn't think he was in *enough* trouble already. Misha just hung his head.

I tried to tell them about the face I had touched in the dark.

Bobbi shook her head. "It was a nightmare. You were asleep."

"No, I wasn't!"

"Well, then it was Jesse's face. Didn't you say he was sitting beside you?"

"On my left! Jesse was sitting on my left! The face was on my right!"

At the sound of his name, Jesse started thrashing around in his goo-pool. Everybody had to stop talking to try to get him out. Man, it was gross. There was hardly a part of him you could touch without getting all glued-up yourself. Pretty soon, Bobbi, Misha, me and the police were all covered in guck.

The police especially were *not* pleased.

"What *is* this stuff?" Bobbi stared at a disgusting orange smear that covered the back of her hand.

I muttered the ingredients.

Her eyes widened. "*Roofing* tar? *Corn* syrup?"

By the end, she was speechless. Looking pale and tired, she dragged Jesse off to take a shower. Misha sank onto a wooden chair and closed his eyes.

Which left *me* to explain my brilliant plan to the police. Under the bright overhead light, with two huge guys in uniform staring down at me, it sounded a little less brilliant. They listened, though – up until the part about the lawn mower.

The one with the moustache sighed. "Okay, this has gone far enough."

The other one took off his glasses and rubbed his eyes. "Young lady, I don't know about Vancouver, but around here we don't mow our lawns in January."

"Yes sir," I said quickly. Rats! I should never have mentioned the lawn mower.

The police gave me and Misha this big lecture about responsibility and how much wild-goose chases like this cost the taxpayers and a bunch of other stuff I can't remember. Before they left, the one wearing glasses pointed a finger at Misha.

"We'll talk to *you* again in the morning."

Misha turned pink and nodded, staring at the floor.

Then they were gone.

I glanced over at Misha. He didn't move.

"Hey, Misha? I'm ... really sorry."

He still didn't move.

"I guess I've made things even worse for you?" I waited for him to say, Don't worry about it, no problem.

He didn't.

"Misha, I, uh – "

He gave me a look like he'd just seen his pet dog run over. "Look, Stevie, forget it. Just go to bed, okay?"

I put my jacket and boots on slowly, in case he changed his mind and wanted to talk.

He didn't.

I found Jesse and Bobbi in the bathroom. Jesse was leaning over the sink and yelling, while Bobbi shampooed his hair.

"If we don't get that stuff out," she was saying, "we'll have to cut off all your hair."

I headed to my bedroom feeling terrible. Might as well face it – my brilliant plan had turned into a nightmare. A disaster. A horror movie. All I'd wanted was to help Misha, and now he was in worse trouble than ever. By noon tomorrow, he'd probably be in jail. Jesse would be as bald as a golf ball. And what did we have to show for it?

Nothing.

Only a mysterious face I *thought* I had touched in the middle of the night.

Misha was right.

I *was* a pea brain.

CHAPTER

THERE'S NOTHING WORSE THAN WAKING UP IN THE morning to a mistake left over from the night before. It took me a couple of seconds to remember. Then I groaned and pulled the covers over my head, blocking out the polka-dot curtains of the spare room. Maybe I could go back to sleep and not wake up till next Sunday, an hour before flight time.

"Stevie! You awake?" Jesse's voice from the hall.

I remembered his middle-of-the-night shampoo. "Jesse?"

"Yeah?"

"Do you still have hair?"

Silence. Then, "Of course, I have hair. Come on, Stevie, Bobbi wants us to clean up the greenhouse."

The greenhouse. The goo-pool. I groaned again. Now I *really* wanted to go back to sleep.

"Stee-veee! Come on!"

Did you ever see one of those old movies of prisoners working on a chain gang? Well, that was Jesse and me for the next two hours. We started with egg flippers and dust pans, scraping gobs of goo into plastic containers. Bobbi had given us rubber gloves, but the fingers all stuck together. So we used our bare hands, which got covered in guck after one scrape. Jesse couldn't stand it. He kept washing his hands in a sink in the corner. He could get most of the stickiness off but not the colour. Something in that goo stained our hands bright orange.

"Where's Misha?" I asked after the first hour. "How come he isn't helping?"

"He's at the police station," said Jesse, "trying to explain."

"Oh." I scraped harder.

After a while, we moved on to old rags and newspapers and the cleaning liquid Bobbi said would help soak up the goo.

"Not bad," she said, when she came to check things out. "Be sure you clean up the footprints behind that table, too. Honestly, Jesse, if I'd had any idea – "

"Don't worry, Bobbi," Jesse interrupted. "By the time we're through, this place will shine."

Shine? I gave him a nudge. Getting things to shine is *hard*, and to tell you the truth, I'm not that interested. It's like when I clean my room at home. My mom wants it to be clean-enough-to-eat-off-the-floor. I'm happy with clean-enough-to-*see*-the-floor.

The rags worked pretty well, except that we needed a lot of them. As we scrubbed and rinsed and scrubbed again, Jesse asked about the face. "Did you *really* feel it, Stevie? Or were you dreaming, like me?"

I sat back on my legs to think. "It was real, Jesse. I'm ninety-five per cent sure. I mean, if I put out my hand right now, I can almost feel it." Holding out an orange hand, I couldn't help shuddering.

Jesse gave a little shudder, too. "What kind of face was it?"

I shrugged. "It had a mouth, a nose, skin – "

"Smooth skin? Rough? Bumpy?"

"You think I took the time to *feel* it?"

"I was just wondering if it was a man or a woman. Men's faces are usually rougher – from shaving."

"Oh." Good thinking. Better thinking than mine, actually. Maybe I really *was* losing it.

Closing my eyes, I tried to remember. Cool skin and something else – a soft wetness. "I think I must have touched it high up, Jesse. I think I may have poked it in the eye."

"Uggh." He winced.

"What I don't understand is – how did the thief miss our trap? It's right in front of the door."

Jesse thought. "I don't know, unless – maybe he *didn't* miss it. Maybe he got one foot into the goo and figured out what it was and stepped back."

"Yeah, but then he'd have left footprints."

We stared at each other.

"FOOTPRINTS!" we yelled together.

We raced behind the table to see the footprints that Bobbi had told us to clean up. A trail led from the goo-puddle to where Jesse and I had been sitting the night before. The marks were pretty faint – the kind only a grandma, or maybe a mom, would notice, which explains why Jesse and I hadn't spotted them before. They were browny-orange and really faint against the grey concrete of the floor, but they were all the same – the sole of a right boot.

"Are you sure they're not *your* footprints?" I asked Jesse.

"No way, Stevie. You saw. As soon as I got out of the goo-pool, I went straight into the house with Bobbi."

I thought hard. Maybe one of the police officers had tracked goo back here? Or me? Or Misha? No matter how hard I tried, though, I couldn't remember any of us leaving the area beside the door. These marks *had* to have been made by the thief. Obviously, he – or she – had stuck one foot into the trap and then pulled back.

A wave of excitement moved through me. These prints were our first real break. If I was right, they were the key to the whole case.

"Do you know what these footprints are?" I said. "They're evidence. If we can match them with a pair of boots or shoes, we've got our thief."

"Wow!" Jesse stared. "Finally! Real evidence. Something we can show the police! Wow, Stevie!"

We squatted down to get a closer look.

"I think we could use a magnifying glass," I said.

"Right!" Hustling into his jacket and boots, Jesse raced out the door. Minutes later he returned, pink-cheeked with cold, carrying a magnifying glass and a flashlight.

"Hey, Stevie!" He focused the flashlight on a footprint as I peered through the glass. "This is the real thing, right?"

"What?"

"Detecting. This is real detecting."

"What are you talking about? We've been detectives for over a year now."

"Yeah, but we never had, you know, a real magnifying glass before." Jesse's voice was hushed. "This is, wow, this is just like the Sherlock Holmes books."

"Yeah, well, check *this* out, Sherlock. See here? You can make out the marks really well. A bunch of lines fanning out around the edges and in the middle, a group of circles."

"Yeah, wow, Stevie, I can."

"Jesse?"

"Yeah?"

"Would you do me a favour? Would you stop saying 'Wow'?"

"Oh yeah. Wow, I didn't mean to – "

"Jesse!"

"Okay."

As we peered at the footprints, we saw the same pattern over and over – the edge ringed by lines and the middle part full of circles. I tried putting my right foot over one of the prints.

"What are you doing?" asked Jesse.

"Checking the size."

He peered down. "Big. A man."

The footprint was quite a bit bigger than my foot, which isn't exactly dainty.

"Or a woman with really big feet." I thought for a minute. "Did you ever take a good look at Oliver's feet?"

Jesse shook his head. "Why would I be looking at another guy's feet?"

A half-blurred picture came into my mind – Oliver in the Conservatory cafeteria, slouched low in a plastic chair, blue-jeaned legs stretched out, feet resting on another chair. His boots were brown, I remembered. Leather. Laced up to the ankle and kind of dressy-looking, like the rest of Oliver's clothes. But the size? And the pattern on the soles? That's where it got blurry.

"Time for another trip to Oliver's house," I said. "*This* time we're looking for boots."

We dressed quickly and headed for the house to tell Bobbi where we were going. Coming in the back door, we heard voices in the kitchen. One was Bobbi's. But the other?

Veda Bickel.

She was sitting at the table with Bobbi, a cup of coffee in her hand. Huge, dark glasses covered her eyes. She was wearing a baggy blue sweatshirt and a pair of black tights that made her legs look about five metres long. She was also wearing the one thing I'd never expected – a smile.

"Finished so soon, kids?" Bobbi asked. "Come in, and make yourselves a sandwich. Have you met Veda? Yes, of course. You went to the last meeting of the club. Sorry to interrupt, Veda. You were saying?"

"What's *she* doing here?" Jesse whispered in my ear.

Putting a finger to my lips, I walked quietly over to the kitchen counter, where Bobbi had left out some lunch things. Jesse followed, and the two of us started automatically smearing stuff onto bread, listening hard. Do you know that expression about being "all ears"? Mine felt like satellite dishes. It took every bit of their hearing power to make out Veda's voice, which had dropped to a hush.

"... feeling bad about the way I treated Misha at the last meeting. A couple of the other members spoke to me later, reminding me that there hadn't been a trial or even an arrest and, of course, they were right. Innocent until proven guilty. I've thought about it and decided that I was probably being a bit unfair. I – " A pause. I saw her glance in our direction. "I don't get along very well with young people, you see."

"I understand," said Bobbi, nodding.

"But I'm certainly not an ogre. I wouldn't want anyone to think I was persecuting the poor boy."

"Of course not."

"Anyway, I was in this neighbourhood, visiting a friend and – "

And? And what?

But Veda had turned her back. Her voice dropped to a mumble, and I couldn't hear a thing. Slapping my sandwich onto a plate, I dashed for the chair beside Bobbi.

"... wasn't home, so I thought I'd drop in here."

Bobbi's voice was soothing. "Well, that's very nice, Veda. And I certainly appreciate ... uh, Stevie?"

I looked up. "Yes?"

"What *is* that in your sandwich?"

I glanced down. Something dark and grainy. I opened the sandwich.

Bobbi stared. So did Veda.

Great. A coffee-grounds sandwich.

Think fast, Stevie.

"Too tall," I said.

"Beg your pardon?" said Bobbi.

"I'm getting too tall. I heard coffee stunts your growth."

Another silence – even longer this time. Bobbi stared at the sandwich like it was a live hedgehog.

Oh boy. Wait till Misha heard about *this*.

"I'm glad we, er, had this chance to talk," said Veda, still staring at the sandwich as she got up. Bobbi stood, too. "And now, if you have a moment, I'd love to see Misha's new plants."

"His what?" said Bobbi.

Uh, oh.

"Misha's new plants – the ones that were delivered yesterday," said Veda. "Muffy told me all about them. It sounds like he received some exciting new specimens."

Bobbi sucked her breath in hard. "Stevie? Jesse? Do *you* know anything about this?"

It's at moments like this that I remember an old expression my dad sometimes quotes: "Oh, what a tangled web we weave when first we practise to deceive." This web was tangled all right. And it was getting more snarled up every second. Jesse and I started babbling confused half-answers. I couldn't help thinking of Misha. This was going to look like even *more* proof that he was a liar. And it was all my fault. Again!

"Perhaps I'd better go," Veda said finally, shaking her head in confusion. Bobbi followed her to the front hall.

As soon as they were gone, Jesse darted to my side. "Did you *see*, Stevie?"

"See what?" I was too busy feeling crummy to see anything.

"Veda's feet. They're huge! Way bigger than yours or mine."

I sighed. Jesse had a habit of leaping to conclusions, but this was a bit much, even for him. "Just because a person has big feet," I said, "doesn't mean she's a thief."

"Oh, no? Well, what about her dark glasses?"

Her glasses? Now he'd *really* lost me.

"Remember what you said about poking the thief in the eye? A poked eye would look red and sore, right? And a person with a sore, red eye might want to hide it. Dark glasses, right?"

Was it possible? Could it have been Veda's face in the dark last night?

"Stevie, she's getting away. Her *boots* are getting away. We have to stop her!"

I was moving, I noticed, towards the kitchen door. The funny thing was – I wasn't walking. Jesse had his hands on my back. He was actually *pushing* me through the kitchen door.

"Stop!" I snapped, grabbing the frame as I slid by.

I couldn't believe it. He was still pushing. This was *his* idea and *his* suspicion. How come *I* was the one going through the door?

"Will you cut it out!"

He dropped his hands, surprised.

"If you're so curious, why don't *you* check Veda's boots?"

He shrugged. "I'm no good at that stuff."

"What stuff? Looking at boots? Or acting like an idiot?"

"Aw, Stevie."

"How come I always have to get in trouble and look like the dingbat, Jesse? How come – "

Slam.

The sound of the front door closing shut both of us up. We flew down the hall together, arriving at the front door just in time to watch Veda drive off.

"Nice of her to drop by," said Bobbi, giving a final wave. "Ready for lunch, you two?" She grinned. "Something a little more nutritious than coffee sandwiches maybe? I'll make tuna melts."

As we followed Bobbi back to the kitchen, Jesse whispered, "We lost her, Stevie." But the way he said it, I could tell he really meant, "*You* lost her."

I thought about arguing.

Nah. Only a pea brain would argue.

"Don't worry," I told him. "Veda isn't our prime suspect anyway. We have bigger fish to fry."

"Fish? You mean the tuna melts?"

Sometimes it's awfully hard to be Jesse Kulniki's partner.

"Oh," he said finally, figuring it out. "You mean Oliver."

I nodded. "Oliver. It's time we got a really good look at that guy's feet!"

CHAPTER

13

"OLIVER'S NOT HOME," SAID MARY BETH, "BUT HE should be back really soon." She peeked out at Jesse and me, shivering on her front step. It had started to snow as we walked over, and large white flakes drifted slowly past our faces, grabbing onto eyebrows, eyelashes and any hair that wasn't under a hat. "Want to come in? You could help me look for Sigmund some more."

"Sure," I said. It would be a chance to warm up. And maybe Oliver would come back.

So there we were *again,* hunting for a hamster who had probably chewed his last Kibble Nibble at least three days before. It was getting harder to pretend – and even harder to listen to Mary Beth's sweet, hopeful voice. "I'm sure he's here *somewhere.*"

"Tell her!" hissed Jesse.

"Tell her what?" I hissed back. "That her brother's a crook? That her hamster is plant food?"

Somewhere in the middle of the fake hamster hunt, I had the bright idea of doing a real search – for Oliver's boots. I turned the front hall closet upside-down, but the closest I came was a pair of red running shoes. Mary Beth said Oliver used them for basketball. They were about the right size. They were also incredibly smelly, and soon I was practically gagging on the fumes. One of those not-fun moments in detecting. There seemed to be more and more of them lately.

Jesse showed up to report that he couldn't get into Oliver's room. It looked like Oliver wasn't taking any more chances – the door was locked. We hung around for another twenty minutes or so, hoping Oliver would show up, but no luck.

Mary Beth's chin trembled as we left. "I'll keep looking," she said. "Sigmund *has* to be somewhere in the house."

"Poor Mary Beth," said Jesse, as we trudged home through the falling snow.

"It'll be hard to explain at school," I agreed. When the other kids heard about the ghastly way little Sigmund had met his end, they would *not* be pleased.

As we tramped along, my mind drifted back over the last twenty-four hours. Things had not gone well. The greenhouse disaster. The coffee grounds sandwich. Then, suddenly, it hit me – whack! – like a snowball in the face. I stopped dead.

"Hurry up, Stevie. It's freezing out here."

"Jesse! Do you remember what Veda said this morning? About visiting someone in the neighbourhood?"

He nodded. "Something about a friend who wasn't home." The words were hardly out of his mouth when his eyes shot wide open. "Oh my gosh! Do you think Veda's friend was *Oliver*?"

"He's in the neighbourhood, isn't he? And he's not home."

Jesse thought. "Wait a second. Are you saying that Oliver and Veda are in this together?"

I shrugged. "*She* knows plants. And *he* could get Old Pete. It sounds crazy, but – " I stopped, trying to wrap my mind around the idea.

Veda? And Oliver? Partners?

"It wouldn't be the first time we've come across a strange pair of partners in crime," said Jesse.

He was right. In a bizarre crime like this, anything was possible. The secret to solving a mystery, I'd learned from hard experience, was to keep your mind open.

I started walking again, quickly. "Okay. Let's say they *are* partners. Which one was in the greenhouse last night? Remember, there was only one kind of footprint."

"So what?" Jesse danced along sideways beside me, his boots kicking up snow. "They could *both* have been in the greenhouse, Stevie. The one who put a boot in the goo could have warned the other one. Or maybe one stayed outside, standing guard."

I nodded. It was all possible. Strange, but possible.

But wait. If Veda *had* broken into the greenhouse last night, why would she come over to Bobbi's house today?

"That's easy," said Jesse, when I asked. "She was returning to the scene of the crime."

Hmmm. I'd heard that, too – that some criminals couldn't stop themselves from going back to the place where they'd committed a crime. It was almost funny when you thought about it. I imagined some criminal, the day after a crime, brushing his teeth maybe or eating his cereal, thinking happy thoughts of how he's going to spend his loot. All of a sudden, he looks down, and what's this? His feet are moving. They're walking outside. The criminal freaks out. But what can he do? He can't stop his feet from carrying him, step by horrible step, *back to the scene of the crime.*

Was that how it was for Veda?

"Thank goodness for those footprints," said Jesse. "All we have to do is match them with a pair of boots, and we've got it made."

I nodded. "We're really close, Jesse. I can feel it in my bones."

Bobbi called out from the living room as we stepped inside. We found her slumped on the couch, looking tired and unhappy. Beside her feet was the bucket of cleaning supplies we had used on the goo-pool.

"Jesse? Stevie? I thought we had a deal. You promised to clean up the mess in the greenhouse."

Jesse and I stared at each other, confused. "We did," said Jesse. "We scraped the floor and then washed it, just like you told us to. Didn't we, Stevie?"

"Well, you did a good job on the puddle. But you left all those footprints. It took me an hour to scrub them off."

"WHAAAT!" I screeched.

"Bobbi, no!" cried Jesse. "They were evidence!"

"Evidence!" Bobbi rolled her eyes. "I hate to say it, Jesse, but I think I'm going to have to fire my own grandson. Waking me up in the middle of the night, making me scrub stinky goo all afternoon – "

"Bobbi, I'm sorry, but you don't understand." Jesse was talking so fast, he was practically babbling. "Those footprints were important. We *needed* them."

Closing her eyes, Bobbi massaged her forehead. "My headache is getting *much* worse," she said. "I'm going to lie down, and I do *not* – I repeat, not – want to be disturbed."

After she left, Jesse and I collapsed onto the couch.

"Perfect!" I said. "Just great! After days of work, we finally find a clue. And what happens? Some neat-nut goes swish with a mop, and goodbye evidence."

"Don't call Bobbi a neat-nut," muttered Jesse. "It's not her fault. She's a grandmother. All grandmothers are neat."

"My grandma isn't!" I snapped. "*My* grandma's house is one big heap of clutter. You know what, Jesse? I think neatness runs in your family."

"Does not!" He looked horribly insulted.

I guess we were both pretty upset. We ended up having this long, stupid argument about neatness that dragged in our families, our rooms, our hair, our handwriting and even what we did with old candy wrappers. Finally, it got really dumb.

"But you're *supposed* to floss your teeth twice a day," said Jesse. "It has nothing to do with neatness."

"Fine," I said. "Can we please just drop it?"

For a couple of minutes, neither of us spoke. Jesse started throwing a cushion in the air and catching it.

Suddenly he stopped. "Stevie? You don't suppose there are *more* footprints – in the snow, maybe, outside the greenhouse?"

I shook my head. "I checked. The snow's all packed down and – JESSE!" I leaped to my feet.

"Wh-what?" he stammered.

"There *are* footprints. And they *are* in the snow. But not here."

"Where, then?"

"Outside Muffy's house. I saw them from her solarium at the meeting. Big holes in the snow from the thief's feet! I forgot all about them."

"Stevie, that was days ago. And it's snowing. Those tracks will be all covered up by now."

"Maybe," I said, "but maybe not. Some of them were underneath an overhanging roof. That snowstorm on the day we arrived hadn't touched them. Lester Potts told me it was because the wind was blowing the wrong way."

Jesse frowned. "I wonder which way the wind's blowing now."

"What wind?"

He pointed out the front window.

A gust of snow rose from a drift in front of the window and whirled in a small circle.

I groaned. "Oh, no."

As if to tease us, a second flurry rose like a tiny tornado from the drift.

"We've got to get over to Muffy's house," I said. "Right now."

"How?" asked Jesse. "Anyway, what's the point? Footprints in the snow aren't like stains on cement. They're way too blurry to be evidence."

"Maybe so. But we can see how long they are – and their shape, and maybe even some markings on the sole. We can see if they were made by the same boot that made the prints in the greenhouse."

His face got more eager with every word. "You're right. We have to check them out. But how?"

I pointed out the front window. Pulling into the driveway was a lime green junker with white fenders and a blood red hood.

"Get your parka on, Jesse. Our ride has arrived."

CHAPTER

"UH, UH. NO WAY. FORGET IT!" MISHA SHOOK HIS head firmly as he stamped the snow off his boots. The shoulders of his parka were sprinkled with snow, and his glasses were all fogged up.

"Aw, Misha, come on. Please?" Jesse and me, together.

"Listen, you two, I just spent the day explaining your *last* pea-brained scheme to the cops. Do you think I'm going to get myself in more trouble?"

I decided to ignore the 'pea-brained.' Taking a deep breath, I spoke in my most mature voice. "There won't *be* any trouble. All we want to do is look at some footprints in the snow. What harm could we do?"

"I don't know," said Misha uncomfortably. He shuffled around, trying to think of some way that Jesse and I (especially me) could mess up again. But staring at a bunch of holes in the snow – how could anybody mess *that* up?

"You'll be right there with us," Jesse reminded him. "What could go wrong?"

"I don't know," said Misha again.

"Pleeeeeeeeeese," I whined. To heck with mature. I was desperate.

In the end, he took us, mostly because he couldn't think of a good reason not to. Also because we wouldn't stop bugging him.

"I must be out of my mind," he kept muttering as we chugged down the snowy highway in Old Pete. We sat in the front seat, Jesse in the middle, watching the windshield wipers swish the snow back and forth. Even though it wasn't dark, Old Pete's headlights were on. So were the lights of other cars we passed.

"I wish you could have seen those footprints in Bobbi's greenhouse," Jesse said to Misha. "You'd be just as excited as we are."

"Yeah, sure," mumbled Misha. You'd think we were talking about the tooth fairy.

He turned the radio on. The car filled with loud static.

Misha groaned and shut it off. "Nothing works in this car. Nothing works in my whole life. I don't know why I even try."

There are times when anything you say is going to be wrong. This was one of them. Jesse and I kept our mouths shut.

I peered past the fuzzy red dice hanging from the mirror. Big flakes of white were flying at the car. Were they falling down or being blown at us sideways? Hard to tell.

We slowed down at a gas station and turned onto the little road that led to Muffy's house. Up till now, the roads were higher than the land around, so the snow drifted off the sides. But this little road had big snowbanks on both sides and was covered with a thin layer of snow. We hadn't gone far before Old Pete pulled to a stop.

"What's the matter?" asked Jesse. "Are we stuck?" I peered out at the snow on the road. It didn't very look deep.

"Oh, maaaaan," moaned Misha. With a huge sigh, he dropped his head onto one arm across the steering wheel. "Nothing *ever* goes right!"

"Misha?" said Jesse.

Silence. Then a gruff mumble. "We're out of gas."

Jesse and I exchanged winces.

After a moment, Misha sat up straight, stared out the window, and sighed. "I *knew* I should have fixed that gas gauge. I knew – oh, what's the point? Look, you guys, there's that gas station at the turn-off, just a kilometre back. I'll be back with gas in half an hour. Are you both dressed warm? Good. Stay here." He flipped the hazard lights on and opened his door.

"Uh, Misha? How far are we from Muffy's house?" I was thinking about the footprints. If the wind was blowing in the right direction, they might be getting snowed over. Half an hour might be too late.

"Not far." Misha stepped outside. "It'll just take a few minutes to drive there when I get back."

"Is it okay if Jesse and I start walking?"

He stared down the road, thinking. "I guess so. This road's a dead end, and there's hardly any traffic. And there are farmhouses along the way if you need to stop. But stick to the side, okay? If you see a car coming, get right off."

He disappeared in the direction of the gas station. Jesse and I headed the opposite way, sticking close to the snowbank on the left side. It was snowing hard, but we could still see if a car was coming.

A couple of farmhouses rose up at the end of long driveways. Mostly, though, the land around us was flat and white, bordered by endless wire fences. I tried to imagine what it must be like in July. Once I had seen a picture of Jesse in a field of wheat. The field had looked like a golden ocean, complete with waves. Jesse said that in summer the prairie looked like a patchwork quilt – yellow canola, blue alfalfa, golden wheat.

On a day like today, it was hard to picture, even for someone with *my* imagination.

The snowflakes skimmed off the nylon surfaces of our parkas, but soon our wool mitts and hats were thick and white. The good news was that my lumpy, puffy clothes were doing their job – keeping my body more or less warm. It was my nose, toes and fingertips that got the worst of it. Soon they were at the tingly-numb stage. I remembered a story I'd read once about an explorer named Scott in Antarctica. For a few fence-lengths, I pretended I was him – braving the frozen elements, sticking my strong jaw fearlessly into wind. It helped.

Suddenly, out of the whiteness, a large, dark house shape loomed.

"Is that it?" asked Jesse.

I squinted through the snow. It was like peering through a drifting white curtain. The only other time we'd been here, it had been dark, and I hadn't gotten a good look at the outside of the house.

"I think so."

Close to the house, connected to it by a fence, was a garage. A scrubby tree held out spindly branches nearby.

"I remember that garage," I said. "When we were here, we parked right in front of it. See? There."

I glanced at the house again. The drapes were closed. Maybe Muffy wasn't home? We hadn't bothered to phone. After all, we were coming to check footprints, not to visit. Now that we were shivering in her driveway, though, a visit didn't sound too bad.

Jesse was obviously thinking the same thing. He headed straight for the front door.

I grabbed his arm to stop him. "Not yet. Let's take a look at the footprints before we go in." I knew if we went inside, we'd *stay* inside.

"Aw, Stevie ..."

"It'll only take a minute."

It took more like twenty. There was no path to the back of the house, and we had to drag ourselves through knee-high snow. The holes we were making looked a lot like the ones we were looking for. Would those old tracks still be there?

My boots were slightly open at the top, leaving plenty of room for snow to drop inside. Soon I felt like I was walking with ice-packs tied to my feet. I grunted and trudged on, using a special step I'd developed. Lift left knee as high as possible. Stick foot out straight ahead. Fall forward onto foot. Repeat with right leg. Jesse, I noticed, was doing the same thing.

Finally, I spotted it. The solarium. Lots of glass,

lots of lights, lots of greenery. And there was the overhang that had protected the footprints. I slogged eagerly towards it.

Stopped. Looked down. Nearly burst into tears.

The holes were gone.

We were too late!

All that was left was a few soft dents in the snow. I stood there, jaws clenched, too mad at myself even to cry. If only I had remembered these prints sooner – yesterday or the day before – *before* the snow had wiped them out. Some things I could blame on bad luck. This was my own stupidity.

Jesse stood, staring at the dents. There was nothing to say.

After a minute, he patted me on the shoulder. "Let's go back."

I nodded, and we started the slow slog back. As we came around the front of the mansion, I half expected to see Old Pete in the driveway. But there was no sign of the car – or Misha, either. If Muffy wasn't home, we were in trouble.

The front door had one of those old-fashioned knockers – a brass lion's head where you have to lift the metal jaw and drop it. After dropping the little jaw a couple of times, I got fed up.

"Hey, Muffy!" I hammered on the door. "Let us in."

The door opened a crack – enough to show two round blue eyes and a bunch of golden curls. Then it flew wide open to reveal Muffy in a bright turquoise velvet jumpsuit.

"Stevie! Jesse! What are you – oh my, just look at you! Why, you're half frozen. Come in, my dears, quickly, quickly!"

It took us a while to get our outdoor clothes off and our mouths thawed out enough to speak. Meanwhile, Muffy filled the air with chatter, babbling dozens of questions and oh-my-ing and oh-dear-ing a lot. She fluttered around us, pulling off scarves and snowy hats, her pink fingernails and gold bracelets flashing.

I hardly heard a word. Too busy noticing how *warm* it was in Muffy's house – how deliciously, gorgeously, magnificently warm. As my last snowy clothes came off, I felt like I'd just landed in Hawaii. It even smelled like Hawaii. Glancing around, I spotted a glass vase full of fresh flowers. Ahhhhhhh ...

Muffy herded us into her gym-sized kitchen and sat us down on high wooden stools beside a counter.

"Right here, yes, that's right. Why, Stevie, your hands are ice cubes. I'll make some hot chocolate and – are you hungry? I'll warm up some cinnamon buns, and – but my goodness gracious, you haven't even told me why you're here."

I wasn't really in the mood for long explanations, but I figured we owed it to her. I told her that we were detectives and that Bobbi had asked us to help Misha. Jesse nodded eagerly, bouncing around on his stool. I admitted that Misha's phone call about the new plants had been a fake – part of a trap to catch the thief. Then I told her about the goo-pool.

"Really? Truly?" Muffy's eyes were as round and blue as blueberries. "A trap, you say? Like the traps in the plants? How absolutely fascinating! And then what?"

I started to tell about the night in the greenhouse, but Jesse couldn't hold back any longer. He leaped off his stool and started re-enacting the whole thing. First he tiptoed across the kitchen, dipping his toe into make-believe goo as he pretended to be the thief. Then he rolled around on the floor, waving his arms and screeching, as he pretended to be me. Next, acting out his own role, he stumbled around with his hands out like Frankenstein and then fell onto his backside. Finally, he muscled out his shoulders, tucked his fingers in his belt, and lectured in a stern, police-type voice.

Muffy loved it. You'd think she was at a movie. The hammier Jesse got, the more she clapped and giggled.

"Ooo, ooo, that's wonderful! Do that part again, Jesse, the part where Stevie bangs into the chair!"

"Excuse me!" I interrupted, shooting a glare at Jesse. We weren't a travelling acting troupe, for heaven's sake. Giving me a sheepish look, he crawled back onto his stool. That's when I took over again, telling Muffy about Veda's suspicious visit that morning and the footprints we'd found in the greenhouse and the other footprints outside Muffy's solarium.

"And so," I finished up, "we came here to have a look." Then I sagged. "But the tracks are all gone now. The snow filled them in."

Muffy clucked sympathetically. "What a shame – and after you've worked so terribly hard and followed all those cues."

"Clues," I said.

The bell on the microwave went, and Muffy started bustling around, fixing the snack. The hot chocolate was sweet. I mean, *sweet*. I saw her drop six spoons of sugar into my cup, and Jesse actually choked on his first sip.

"Bless you," said Muffy. "Too hot?"

"No," croaked Jesse, politely lifting his cup for a second sip.

Next came the cinnamon buns – the biggest, softest, puffiest ones I'd ever seen. Steaming from the microwave, they were shiny with glazed sugar, dotted with raisins and walnuts, and topped with fat blobs of butter. I picked one up, and sugary butter ran down my wrist.

Muffy hopped back up on her stool and leaned across the counter eagerly. "I think it's very odd that Veda visited your house today. After all, she's been so mean to Misha. I must say, I'm even a bit frightened of her myself. And come to think of it – " She paused, one pink-nailed finger over her button mouth. "No, I shouldn't say anything."

"What?" said Jesse, gulping down a bite of bun. "Do you know something about Veda?"

Glancing over her shoulder, as if there might be somebody eavesdropping, Muffy dropped her voice to a whisper. "Well, it's not nice to gossip, of course. But now that I'm part of the investigation – I mean, it's so exciting, this detecting business, isn't it? I feel like I'm sort of a partner – "

Great, I thought. A blueberry muffin for a partner.

"Veda Bickel?" I reminded her.

"Oh, yes, Veda. Well, the day before the theft, she spent ages in my solarium, studying the plants. It was as if she were, well, memorizing them. Honestly, I could hardly shoo her out. Now, she *could* have been figuring out their value, couldn't she? She *could* have been checking to see exactly where the most valuable plants were. What do detectives call that?"

"Casing the joint," I said.

"Yes, that's right. Casing the joint." Muffy smiled, dimples showing. "You two must be awfully clever to be detectives."

Jesse grinned.

"Brave, too. Coming all this way to search for cues in a blizzard."

"Clues," I said automatically. It took a second for her last word to sink in. When it did, I almost fell off my stool.

"Blizzard?" I gulped. "*What* blizzard?"

CHAPTER 15

MUFFY'S CURLY HEAD BOBBED IN SURPRISE. "DIDN'T you hear it on the radio? They've been announcing blizzard warnings for several hours."

"Oh, my gosh!" Jesse leaped to his feet. "Misha!"

He dashed out of the kitchen, heading for the front room. Muffy and I followed. Jesse jerked the thick drapes open and then lurched backwards in shock.

The window was a wall of solid, shifting white. Old Pete could have been three metres in front us and we wouldn't have been able to see it.

"See?" said Muffy.

"Misha," whispered Jesse, his face as white as the scene through the window.

"Oh, now, don't you worry." Muffy gently placed a manicured little hand on each of his shoulders. "I'm sure he's quite safe. If you like, we can phone Beeman's Station. I'll bet Misha's there with Joe Beeman right this minute, waiting for the storm to end."

We followed her past a couple of couches and a vase of flowers to a phone.

"Hello?" she said. "Hello? Dear me, what's wrong?"

I held out my hand and took the phone. No dial tone. Nothing.

"Maybe the blizzard knocked out the phone line," I suggested.

She nodded. "At least it hasn't knocked out the electricity. I'll turn on the radio."

We didn't have to wait long. The radio announcer reported traffic grinding to a halt all over the city, bus routes closed – and a few phone lines down.

"We can't even phone Bobbi," wailed Jesse.

"It's okay, Jesse. We left her a note, telling her where we were going. She'll know we're here at Muffy's."

Muffy nodded. "Come back to the kitchen," she coaxed. "Have some more hot chocolate. It'll do you good."

The *last* thing I needed was more hot chocolate, but I figured I'd better be polite. Muffy brought the radio into the kitchen and set it up on the counter. Not that we could hear anything. As usual, Muffy was yakking non-stop, telling us every single detail of some dumb blizzard that had happened when she was a kid.

"It was the March 4 blizzard. No, wait, March 3. I can never remember. Maybe it was March 4. No, March 3. Anyway, I could see the snow falling as soon as I woke up. I was wearing my pink flannel nightie, I remember ... or was it the blue one? And ..."

Jesse wasn't listening. He was slumped over the counter, looking worried and upset.

There wasn't much to do except eat. I wolfed down two more cinnamon buns and three more cups of hot chocolate. I didn't stop till I noticed that my teeth were getting fuzzy. By that time, I was starting to feel a little icky in the stomach, too. I peeled off a sweater. Sure was stuffy in there, and the sickly-sweet smell of the flowers only made things worse.

Muffy was still telling her blizzard story, going on and on about how glad her teacher had been to see her when she finally arrived at school.

"I was always Mrs. Kirgenblass's favourite student, and that day I was going to recite a poem. Something about tulips in the spring. Let me see, I think I can still recite – "

Tulips in the spring?

Time for a break!

"Where's the bathroom, Muffy?"

Looking disappointed, she shrugged and gave me directions.

It took me about a minute to get lost.

"Some detective you are!" I muttered to myself. "First you lose two sets of footprints. Then you can't find your way to the bathroom. Excellent work, Stevie Diamond."

But maybe getting lost wasn't such a bad thing. At least it got me away from Muffy's chatter. I climbed a wide, thickly carpeted staircase and wandered down a long, dark hall. Then, passing a bunch of doors, I got curious. What did Muffy do with all these rooms? Might be fun to try to guess. The first one was easy. It was set up with a sewing machine and lots of piles of fabric, most of it in Muffy-type colours – pink and peach and baby blue. The next three were bedrooms, the biggest obviously Muffy's. It was white and blue – a princessy-looking room, full of lace and silky bits and ribbons. Half of one wall was covered with a painting of a beaming, blue-eyed little girl with long, golden ringlets. Except for getting her hair cut, Blueberry Muffy had hardly changed a bit.

I wandered on to a large room with a fireplace and a couple of comfy couches facing one of those giant-screened TVs. Why couldn't Muffy invite us in *here* instead of keeping us stuck in her kitchen? And why couldn't she make us some *real* food – like nachos or hot dogs – something without sugar? Man, I was feeling grumpy. Why was it so darned hot in this house, anyway?

And where the heck was the bathroom?

When I opened the next door, I thought I'd stumbled into the solarium. Plants everywhere. But this room wasn't round, and it didn't have glass walls. And *these* plants didn't look like the ones I had seen in the solarium.

They were flowers. Gorgeous flowers with purple, pink, yellow and red blossoms. Like the ones in the vase downstairs except that there must have been hundreds of them here in little individual pots. Scattered around the walls and ceiling were powerful lights.

What on earth?

Stepping inside, I gazed around. I thought back to Muffy's nattering. Maybe I'd missed the part where she talked about growing flowers?

What were these anyway? They were all the same kind – just different colours. And I'd seen them before – but where? After staring at a big purple blossom for a second, I remembered.

My mom has this old photo album from when she's a kid, and every now and then, when I'm *extremely* bored, I look through it – mostly so I can have a laugh at how kids used to dress in the olden days. Somewhere near the end was a close-up of my mom at her high school graduation dance. She was wearing this thing she called a "corsage." It's really just a fancy flower that you pinned to your fancy dress, but my mom said it was a big deal. Your date had to buy it for you and give it to you in a box. Part of flirting back then, I guess.

Anyway, Muffy's flowers were the same as the ones in my mom's corsage. What was their name? Had an *o* and an *r* in it, I remembered. Oregano? No, that was a herb. Okra? No, that was a vegetable.

Orchids.

Yes! That was it – orchids.

I smiled, extremely pleased with myself. Then another memory drifted in – from the day we visited the Winnipeg Conservatory. My smile slowly faded.

My jaw dropped.

Orchids!

CHAPTER

OKAY, I'LL TELL YOU THE TRUTH. AT THAT MOMENT, I didn't have it all figured out. In fact, in some ways, those orchids just made things more confusing. What I *did* know was what I had to do next.

As soon as I could breathe again, I charged around the room, looking for something – anything – that would tell me whether my suspicions were correct.

I found it on a table, shuffled in among a bunch of gardening magazines. A plain white envelope with an address typed on it:

Mrs. Alicia Flaversham, President
Royal Victorian Exotic Orchid Society
63 Sparrow Knoll Road
Winnipeg, Manitoba

Yes!

I *was* on the right track. But no time now to sit around and figure things out. I'd been gone from the kitchen for at least ten minutes. Muffy and Jesse would start wondering.

Move, Stevie! Racing back down the hall to Muffy's bedroom, I threw open her closet door. The floor was littered with tiny fat shoes, all in heaps. I pawed through them for a minute or two, then dashed out into the hall again. For the next few minutes, I ran from room to room, peering into any closet or cupboard I could find. Then I raced back down the staircase – and got lost all over again. Trying to avoid the kitchen, I went in a circle twice, ending up back at the staircase.

This place was like a maze.

Eventually I found myself in a room with a concrete floor, full of stacked patio furniture and garden hoses and other stuff. A door at one end led outside. Right beside it was a closet. I opened the closet door. Life preservers, umbrellas, old jackets ...

Boots!

Small boots at the front. At the back – *big* boots. Four or five pairs. I picked up a pair of black ones. Right size. Wrong pattern. Then I grabbed a pale brown boot made of leather. I turned it over.

The edge of the sole was – ringed by lines. Yes!

The middle? Full of circles.

I picked up the matching boot and turned it over. Right where the sole met the leather –

An ugly orange stain! Exactly like the stains on my hands from cleaning the greenhouse.

I leaned against the wall and let out all my breath at once. These were *the* boots, no question.

I'd found them.

But *whose* boots were they? They were way too big for Muffy. They looked too big even for me.

I lifted my right foot and stuck it inside the boot. It wouldn't go. Something was in the way. I stuck my hand inside and pulled out –

A shoe! A little fat white running shoe stuffed into the bottom of the boot. I stared in astonishment. Then I stuck my hand in the other boot. Another running shoe!

What???

Then I got it. A person with tiny feet could wear these big boots, but only if she wore *her own little shoes inside.*

"Steeeeveeee ..." Muffy's voice. I froze.

She was looking for me.

Dropping the boots as if they were on fire, I raced out, charged down a hall, and skidded to a halt at the foot of the big staircase. Muffy was standing there, fingernails tapping on the banister.

"Oh, there you are, dear. When you didn't come back, I thought – goodness, Stevie, are you okay? You look all red and puffed out. I was afraid you'd wandered outside or – "

"Um, no," I said quickly. "I'm fine. I just, er, got lost."

Watch it, I told myself. Too many ums and ers. I smiled brightly. "I found the bathroom. It was great. Fantastic toilet. Big, roomy sink. Nice tub. Terrific!"

I was babbling. Shut up, idiot.

Muffy blinked, confused. "Well, that's good, dear. I'm glad you enjoyed yourself. Come along now. I just realized – silly me – I've been feeding you those buns and here it's dinner time. I'm heating up some Chinese food in the microwave. You must be starved!"

"No," I answered truthfully. "Actually I'm not hungry."

"Nonsense," said Muffy, taking my hand and leading me towards the kitchen. Her hand felt small, moist and sticky in mine.

Jesse grinned when he saw me. "Did you fall in, Stevie?"

"Yeah." I tried to smile. "Sure. Fell in."

Fortunately, Muffy was babbling away and didn't pay much attention to me as she set the table. She seemed to be in the middle of telling Jesse some story about a pony her father had given her for her fifth birthday.

"I called him Prince. I guess that's because Mummy and Daddy called *me* their little princess. Of course, I never did ride him much. But he looked adorable in the little stable Daddy had made for him."

I watched the yellow curls dance, the little pink mouth natter, the round blue eyes blink. Muffy looked and acted so dumb.

But she *wasn't!*

She had to be incredibly smart to pull off what I was now positive she had pulled off. I was wracking my brain, and I still didn't have even half of it figured out.

"Stevie?" Jesse's voice. "You okay? You look funny."

"Yeah. Fine." I tried to smile, but it felt like a school-picture smile. Totally fake.

"Dinner!" trilled Muffy.

We ate at the big table. The giant chandelier hung above our heads like a thousand glass daggers waiting to fall. Dinner was sweet-and-sour chicken, but you would have had to search really hard to find the sour. Deep-fried chicken balls, which Jesse had to pick around. Hunks of pineapple, red pepper and carrot floating in a sugary, red sauce. Each bite got stuck halfway down my throat and hung there for three or four swallows before I could get it down.

Worst of all was the heat. Muffy must have cranked it up while I was gone. The room was like a sauna. Jesse had peeled off a couple of layers and was down to a white T-shirt. He looked kind of drowsy. I kept my sweatshirt on. I know it doesn't make sense, but the shirt made me feel safer, even though sweat trickled down my back in itchy rivers.

Gulping down a last mouthful of pineapple, Muffy muttered something about visiting the little girls' room and disappeared. I waited till I heard her shoes tap away into the distance before I spoke.

"Jesse, it's her!"

Burping loudly, he focused his eyes sleepily in my direction. "Her who?"

"Muffy! She's the Orchid Lady."

"The what?" He reached slowly across the table in the direction of a napkin, burping again and giving me a little grin. "Ever notice how pineapple can give you gas?"

I grabbed his arm and squeezed. "Jesse! Pay attention!"

"Oww, Stevie! Cut it out."

"We don't have much time, so you'd better listen." Quickly, I told him about the orchid room and the envelope I had found there. "Do you see what this means?"

"Alicia Flaversham," he repeated, frowning. "The woman in the Conservatory told us that a Mrs. Flaversham was president of the orchid club. But what's that got to do with Muffy?"

"Muffy's real name is Alicia!" I said. "Muffy is just her nickname – she told me herself. I don't know where Flaversham comes from, but I do know one thing. Muffy De Witt and Alicia Flaversham are the same person."

Jesse thought for a second. "So? Why can't she be president of the orchid club *and* a member of the carnivorous plants club?"

"Jesse, don't you see? The two clubs are rivals. Muffy's not interested in carnivorous plants. She just joined the Carnivore Club to mess things up."

Jesse's eyes went huge. "Stevie, are you trying to tell me that *Muffy* is the thief?"

"Yes!" I hissed.

"But she's rich. She doesn't need to sell stolen plants."

"Of course not," I said. "She just stole them to keep the Carnivore Club from putting on their display. She wants her orchid club to get the new wing of the Conservatory."

Jesse's mouth opened into an oval large enough to stick an egg through. "Wow!"

"Yeah, wow."

"Oh, my gosh!" He jerked bolt upright.

"What?"

"Stevie, we're trapped. The blizzard! While you were gone, Muffy told me it could take twenty-four hours to clear the roads. We're going to have to spend the night here. Alone! With her!"

My sugar-coated mouth went dry. "Okay," I said, and then again, "okay. Just don't panic. As long as we act nor– "

"Hssst!" said Jesse, and I heard it. The tap, tap, tap of tiny feet coming down the hall.

CHAPTER

I RE-ARRANGED MY FACE INTO THE CLOSEST I COULD come to a calm, friendly expression. Then I glanced at Jesse.

Uh, oh.

His face was sickeningly pale. His lower lip was actually quivering.

Muffy bustled in carrying plates covered with extra-large slices of raisin pie. She put one in front of Jesse. His mouth opened once, twice, three times – and a single word came out – loud.

"RAISIN!"

Oh, man! I should never have told him about Muffy. Jesse freaks out over a spelling test. How was he going to handle *this?*

Crouching low, he started shovelling pie into his mouth.

"No thanks," I said, when she slid a slice in front of me. "I'm full."

She slapped a fork into my hand. "As my dear mummy used to say, there's *always* room for dessert. Now eat!"

I couldn't help thinking of that fairy tale – the one

where Hansel and Gretel get lost in the woods, and the witch fattens them up to eat them. Raisins were dripping in a sugary goo out the sides of the pie. I was going to throw up – I was sure of it.

"P-PIE!" squawked Jesse out of nowhere.

Muffy frowned. She was definitely looking suspicious now. Suddenly I wondered where she'd gone when she left the kitchen. What had she seen? Had I left the door of the orchid room open? Had I put the boots away?

Something – anything – to distract her!

"Jesse and me, we love pie," I babbled.

The words were hardly out of my mouth when the first bite of pie hit my stomach, and a throw-up feeling rose like lava. The green walls of the kitchen swam. Swollen raisins, flowery smells, horrible heat –

I took quick shallow breaths to fight it down.

But Muffy wasn't looking at me. Her face was tight and mean as her eyes fastened firmly on Jesse. I could almost read her mind. *He* was the weak spot. *He* was the one she would go after.

"Jesse, dear, you're awfully quiet," she said softly. "Tell me about … about Vancouver, where you live."

Jesse gulped so loud you could have heard him in the next room. "Well, uh, not much to tell. There's … mountains, and … ocean. Lots of ocean. With, um, salmon and seals and – "

"Whales," I interrupted, hoping to attract her attention back to me.

"ORCHIDS!" shouted Jesse.

"NO!" I shouted, even louder. "No, he means ORCAS! ORCA whales! They're black and white and live in pods. Right, Jesse?"

"YEAH!" hollered Jesse. "ORCAS! ORCAS!"

Another silence. Muffy chuckled. "My, my. *Orchid* whales, Jesse? *Do* tell me more. You're such a marvellous storyteller, I could listen to you all night. Tell me about these whales, dear."

Letting out a sound somewhere between a whimper and a groan, Jesse slumped sideways in his chair. Muffy smiled. It didn't take a genius to see what she was up to. She was planning on picking away at Jesse's brain to find out exactly what he knew. By the time she finished, he would be a wet, quivering puddle.

I couldn't let her do it.

Taking a deep breath, I blurted it out.

"We know everything."

She grinned. She actually grinned, her little white teeth glittering like the crystals of her chandelier. "*Do* you, now? And what exactly is this *everything* that you know?"

"We know you're Alicia Flaversham, president of the Orchid Society. We know you stole the carnivorous plants out of your own solarium. We know you broke into Bobbi's greenhouse the other night." I paused, breathless, and sucked in the muggy air.

"Oh, myyyyy," trilled Alicia Flaversham–Muffy De Witt. "My, my, my. Aren't you the clever ones! And yet, my dear little amateur detectives, you know nothing. Nothing at all!"

She walked over to a big cabinet, pulled a framed photograph out of a drawer, and shoved it in our faces. A big, round man, a chicken-shaped blonde woman and a little blonde girl with ringlets – Muffy, as a child. I recognized her from the painting upstairs.

"Look!" she said. "Mummy and Daddy. Gladys and Winslow De Witt. Do you *know* who they are?"

Jesse and I stared.

"They are the founders of the Royal Victorian Exotic Orchid Society. They founded it together in 1949. Do you know what it was like to grow orchids in a Winnipeg winter back in those days? Do you think it was *easy?*"

Jesse shook his head vigorously. Definitely not easy.

"It required endless work and determination – not to mention enormous sums of money. Mummy and Daddy devoted their *lives* to the Orchid Society. They wanted the whole world to appreciate and enjoy these exquisite blossoms – the royal family of the plant world."

"Royal family?" I repeated. They were just flowers.

"No other bloom is as delicate or as prized," continued Muffy, her voice breathless. "When the Conservatory began to plan its new wing, I knew it had to be the De Witt Wing. I spoke to the Conservatory people. I told them I would be willing to fund it, to supply all the plants."

She was interrupted by a loud burp from Jesse. Horrified, he slapped his hand over his mouth. But Muffy had hardly noticed.

"And what did those idiots at the Conservatory tell me? That they had decided to dedicate the new wing to – to those disgusting, meat-eating creatures!" Muffy's face gathered into a horrible grimace. "Loathesome, crawling vegetation that gobbles down flies! This – *this!* – instead of the exquisite orchids I had offered."

She glared at me and Jesse. "And do you know why the Conservatory wanted these ghastly carnivores? Do you know *why?*"

Jesse and I stared back, speechless.

"Because of you!" she snapped.

What???

"Children!" She almost spat the word out. "The Conservatory people said that they wanted to appeal to younger people. They wanted *children* to get interested in plants – and carnivores would attract them. Hmmph! What nonsense. Any child with half a brain would be far more interested in orchids than in those revolting flesh-eaters."

Wrong, Muffy, dead wrong, I thought.

"The whole business had to be stopped," she went on. "My husband, Boswell Flaversham, tried to talk me out of it. 'Let it go, Muffy, dear,' he said. 'Let them have their silly carnivore wing.' Well! I wasn't listening to *that* sort of talk – and certainly not from my own husband. I shifted old Boswell right out the door. And good riddance! Now I can devote all my time to the De Witt Wing."

Is she nuts, I wondered. How could anybody get this worked up over flowers?

"The hardest part was attending those dreadful meetings at the Carnivore Club. Ill-mannered clods – they don't even know how to pick up a teacup properly. They tie their *napkins* around their necks! Now, at the Orchid Society, we get refined people, people of taste and culture ..." Muffy stared, misty-eyed, at the doorway, as if a bunch of refined, elegant people were about to walk in.

They didn't.

And *I'd* heard enough. "You should have listened to Boswell, Muffy. Your plan isn't going to work."

Her pink lips curled into a smirk. "Oh, no? And why not, my dear? Are you going to make another pool of *pancake syrup* to trap me in?"

I blushed. It did sound pretty dumb.

"Look around." Muffy waved a plump hand at the green walls, the shuttered windows, the howl of the blizzard outside. "*You're* the ones in a trap."

I glanced around. My stomach did its strongest heave yet.

She was right.

I realized something else, too. Jesse and I had tried to imitate a carnivorous plant trap, and we'd done okay. But Muffy? Without even trying, she had done a *way* better job than we ever could have. This place felt *exactly* like the trap of a carnivorous plant. The sticky, sugary foods, the heat, the sweet smells – this must be just what it felt like at the bottom of a pitcher plant.

And Jesse and I? No question. We were Joe and Josephine Insect! A couple of flies, floundering around in a sweet, hot, sticky trap. With a whole new flip of my stomach, I pictured the hours ahead. Jesse and I exhausted, desperate, terrified. Muffy smirking, feeding, heating, waiting …

She smiled now, the corners of her mouth turning up like tiny tendrils. "You are *not* going to spoil my plans," she said.

I stared at Jesse. He stared back.

But not for long.

Because that's when all the lights went out.

CHAPTER

OUT OF THE DARKNESS CAME A GASP. THEN A squeal.

Jesse? Muffy?

It was weird and strange, yet familiar, too. Then I realized why. This was like a replay of the night in the greenhouse, that horrible night when I'd grabbed a face in the dark, and the whole place went berserk.

"Rotten blizzard!" Muffy's voice burst out of the darkness. It was followed by a bang, as if she had pounded the table with her hand.

Quietly, being careful not to scrape my chair, I got to my feet. Following the wooden table with my hands, I began to edge around to Jesse. It's different this time, I reminded myself. That night in the greenhouse, Jesse and I were sleepy. Muffy had the advantage of surprise. This time, we were wide awake. The darkness would be our friend – I hoped.

My hand, groping along the table, touched Jesse's arm. With a wild shriek, he jerked away.

"Jesse, it's me," I hissed.

"*There* you are," Muffy muttered. "Stay where you are. Don't move!"

Okay. New rule. No more talking. Reaching out again, I grabbed Jesse's arm. My other hand found his mouth, and I placed one finger across his lips to signal him to be quiet.

He got it. I jerked at his arm. I guess he understood, because he took my hand and followed me.

It was very creepy. I couldn't even *see* the hand I was holding out in front of me. I was sweating, partly from the heat, but also partly out of fear that my hand would touch that horrible thing it had touched once before in the dark – Muffy's face. After what seemed like an hour, I finally bumped into something solid and flat. The wall. I edged along in the direction of the door. Would Muffy be standing there, waiting?

Gripping the door frame, I took a deep breath and plunged my hand through the doorway. Nothing. Squeezing Jesse's hand, I pulled him through. We were in the hallway.

Behind us came the voice. "Where *are* you? Where are you going?" I heard the unmistakeable sound of a tiny foot stamping.

"I *want* the De Witt Wing," hissed Muffy, "and I am going to *get* it! My husband couldn't stop me. The Carnivore Club couldn't stop me. Do you think a couple of rude little ragamuffins like you are going to stop me?"

Ragamuffins?

What the heck was a ragamuffin, anyway? And even if we were whatever-they-were, what right did a blueberry muffin have to insult a ragamuffin?

I kept moving.

"I will *not* be thwarted." Muffy's voice was shrill and slightly hysterical. "I will *not*. Little brats!"

I shook my head. Who was the brat here, anyway? I had never seen – excuse me, heard – such spoiled-brat behaviour in my life. Muffy was like a two-year-old who always got her way.

Suddenly a soft glow lit up the kitchen behind us. I turned. Outlined in the glow of a candle was a round, yellow face. Muffy's face. Jesse and I shrank back into an alcove. The flickering candle-light danced back into the kitchen, leaving the hall in darkness again.

Safe. For now. But there were two things I knew for sure. One, Muffy and her candle would be back. And two, we had to get away. No way I was going to spend the whole night with the Human Pitcher Plant.

I pulled Jesse deeper into the dark hallway, my hand leading the way like a bug's antenna – reaching, touching, feeling, searching for doorways, stairways, furniture – anything that might tell me where we were.

"Stevie! Where are we going?" Jesse's whisper behind me.

"Shhhh!"

We reached the grand stairway.

Suddenly, I knew where we had to go. The patio-furniture storage room. The one with the door that led outside.

I turned left. There were doors all along here, but I couldn't see into the rooms. How would I find the right one? Thinking hard, I remembered garden hoses, just inside the door, on the right. All I had to do was reach inside, feel for the hoses, and I'd know.

I did it. Room after room – three, four, five. I opened doors, felt around inside and backed out again, edging my way along the curving hall.

"Stevie, what are you doing?"

"Shhhh."

Six, seven. It couldn't be this far, could it? Suddenly the wall ended. I moved out into space, my hand in front, and touched –

The staircase.

I groaned. We had come in a complete circle.

Not only that. The sudden lightening of the gloom behind us could mean only one thing – Muffy and her candle were on our trail. Jesse was digging the fingers of both hands into the top of my arm.

Okay. So I must have made a mistake with the garden hoses. Could they have been on the *left* side of the door?

We started shuffling down the hall again. This time, I reached to the left of each door. At the fourth door, I felt it. Coiled rubber. Garden hoses!

Now we'd have to be *really* careful. This room had at least a hundred terrific noise-makers in it. Clattery metal lawn furniture heaped up in shaky piles. Screened windows leaning against the walls. Buckets filled with garden tools. The whole room was a giant booby-trap – an ear-splitting crash just waiting to happen. Jesse and I would have to move as carefully as if we were on a tightrope.

"Stay right behind me," I whispered, "and don't touch a thing." Holding one hand out in front of me, I inched along, step by tiny step. Twice I felt the edge of a clangy pile of furniture and gently eased around. Once my foot hit a rake. I grabbed it before it could fall. Jesse followed as if he were glued to me.

Finally, we reached the closet. I could tell because my hands suddenly filled with jacket material. I put a hand out to the right and touched cool wood. Yes! – the door to the outside.

"Find a parka," I whispered. "There are boots down below."

"Are you crazy? There's a blizzard out there."

"We only have to get as far as the garage." The way I saw it, we could probably spend the night there. It would probably even be heated. *Everything* seemed to be heated in Winnipeg, and Muffy was especially fond of cranking up the temperature.

I found a big, padded parka with a giant, furry hood and slipped it on. A whole new over-heated, throw-up feeling lurched through me. Ugh. If I didn't get outside fast, I'd be chucking up second-hand raisins. Feeling around the bottom of the closet, I grabbed a bunch of little shoes and boots – all Muffy's, and too small. Then I reached farther into the closet, where I had found *the* boots earlier.

My hands groped at some big boots. Must belong to Boswell Flaversham, the booted-out husband.

"Thanks, Bos," I muttered as I slipped a couple on and handed a couple more to Jesse. From the grunts and swishes I could tell he was putting on a parka, too.

"Stevie!" hissed Jesse. "We need mitts."

Right. Mitts. I reached into my parka pockets – empty. Quickly, I searched through the pockets of other jackets and found leather gloves and a pair of suede mitts.

I handed the mitts to Jesse. The room got slightly brighter as I slipped on the gloves. I could see to do up the jacket. Good.

No! *Not* good. The brightness was coming from a candle. There, in the doorway, stood Muffy De Witt, cheeks and curls glowing in the candlelight.

"Going somewhere, children?"

I grabbed the door, opened it and ran – bang – straight into another door. I pushed at it, but it was stuck. Frozen stuck?

"Jesse, help me," I yelled.

Muffy was threading her way quickly through the piled-up furniture, her candle held high in front of her.

Time to *move!*

"One! Two!" I yelled. "And three!" On three we both threw our weight against the door. It opened – about half a metre. Now I could see why it was stuck.

Snow. Piled up at least waist-high. A gust of wind blew a blast into our faces. Glancing back, I saw Muffy's candle flickering closer.

"Let's *do* it!" I yelled and threw myself out into the snow.

"Out of my waaaay!" shrieked Jesse and threw himself directly on top of me.

I was waist-deep in snow, my face was totally buried, and a hundred pounds of boy was scrambling across my back.

None of that mattered.

Joe and Josephine Insect were free!

CHAPTER

19

"JESSE, FOR CRYING OUT LOUD, WILL YOU – "

"Run, Stevie! Run!"

The blowing snow made it almost impossible to see. As near as I could tell, Jesse had landed waist-deep in a large snowdrift. His arms and legs were churning like windmills, but he didn't seem to be going anywhere.

The snow flying around me suddenly gleamed yellow. I turned. Muffy's face was right in the doorway, huge in the candle's glow. I slammed the door – hard!

Dark. Again.

But a new dark. A white dark, filled with whirling, shifting, driving snow. A dark we could get lost in faster than the dark of the house. A wild, cold darkness made even more scary by the shrieking wind that whistled through it.

"Stevie?"

"Stay close to the wall, Jesse. Follow me."

We had to lift our feet waist-high to walk. Slowly, we made our way along the side of the house. I sucked in the cold air eagerly, turning my face into the snowy blast. After that sweltering house, it felt like a cool shower.

Somewhere along here, I knew, was a wire fence that led to the garage. I almost missed it, but Jesse spotted it at the first corner.

"Over here, Stevie." He veered away from the house.

We followed the fence for fifteen or twenty steps, our legs lifting and dropping like plungers, before the garage loomed out of the whiteness. Jesse whooped out loud and smacked its wall.

"Stevie, we found it!"

He led the way around to the front where the pull-up car door was. Snow had been driven high against it, of course. We had to dig way down, getting icy snow up the wrists of our jackets. Finally we found the handle.

"Pull!" I yelled.

Jesse grabbed on, and we pulled together. The door didn't budge.

"It's locked," yelled Jesse.

Locked? It couldn't be. We tried again.

It was.

"Maybe there's another door," I said. "A regular one."

It took about fifteen minutes to struggle around the garage and find a second door.

"Locked!" moaned Jesse again.

We threw ourselves at this door five or six times, hoping maybe it was just stuck. Finally, we both plopped down in the snow.

Jesse leaned over to shout in my ear. "What now, Stevie? Should we go back?"

Back? Back into that hot, green trap? I felt the sick feeling rise again.

"I can't," I told him.

"Well, we can't stay out here. People *die* in blizzards, Stevie. Haven't you read those pioneer books?"

I knew the ones he meant. Pioneer books always had a blizzard or two in them. Somebody always lost their way in the storm and nearly died. The cows were always starving, too, and somebody had to save them by following the clothesline to the barn.

A clothesline! We didn't have a clothesline, but –

"Jesse, listen! This fence. It keeps going, past the garage. It runs beside the road, remember?"

"Yeah!" Jesse grabbed my arm eagerly. "It goes – hey, Stevie, doesn't it go right to the neighbour's house?"

I nodded. No way we could get lost with a fence to hang onto. I lurched to my feet. "Let's go."

"Hey, Stevie?"

"Yeah?"

"Is it far?"

"No," I said, "not far."

I didn't *think* it was far.

We started out – me heading straight into the wind, and Jesse behind, stepping into my footprints the second I stepped out of them. We both kept our left hands firmly on the fence. Step by slow step, we struggled through the drifts. Soon my hands were like blocks of wood inside their leather gloves. My nose was frozen, too. I couldn't even tell if it was running. I didn't care.

Think about something else, I told myself. Think about Muffy. She had confessed! We knew who had stolen the plants. We also knew why. What we didn't know was *how*.

She must have snuck them out of her house that night – no way she'd take the chance of the police spotting them in another room. But how did she take them away? The neighbours didn't see any cars except Misha's on the road. That's why Misha was the prime suspect. Somehow Muffy had set him up. But how? How had she gotten Old Pete onto that road that night?

My mind raced on. If Muffy was the thief, then she was the one who broke into Bobbi's greenhouse the night Jesse and I set the trap. But I was *positive* no car had driven down Bobbi's road that night. So how had Muffy gotten to Bobbi's house and home again? She couldn't have walked. It was at least ten kilometres each way.

I pulled the hood closer around my face. Something – the thinking maybe, or the cold – was giving me a headache.

"Steeeeveeeee!" Jesse's voice was a wail behind me.

"What?" I had to twist my whole body at the waist to see him.

He was collapsed against the fence. "I can't do this, Stevie. How *far* is it?"

"Not far. Come on, Jesse."

I couldn't help noticing, though, that "far" has a

different meaning when you're dragging a pair of ten-ton boots through waist-high snow. "Far" feels different when a million ragged snowflakes are diving at your face and the wind is shrieking like a caged witch in your ears.

Each step now was a killer. A backbreaking lift of one foot out of its deep snow-hole. Then a giant heave forward, up over the drift, to plant the foot in a new hole. Then the other foot. And the other, and the other, and the other. After a while, I was counting each footstep. How many footsteps to the next house?

Nasty, ugly cold out there in that wind.

How far is far?

Too far.

A dozen more exhausting steps, then, "Steeeveee."

"What?"

"I need to rest. Just for a minute. Just have to close my eyes and ..."

No! That was exactly what happened in the pioneer books. People stopped to rest, they got all sleepy and then, next thing you knew they were dead. Pioneer Popsicles!

"Jesse, you can't. Never, never, *never* go to sleep in a blizzard. It's rule number one in the books."

"Don't care," said Jesse, sagging against the fence. "Just for a minute ..."

A chill went through me that had nothing to do with the snow. Suddenly, I realized we might not make it. If Jesse refused to move, if he went to sleep, what could I do? I couldn't drag him along. I could hardly keep going myself.

We'd be stuck. We'd freeze!

I don't know how long I stood there, frantic, trying to think. At some point, my mind drifted. An image of summer days in Vancouver. Hot sun, green grass. And then I could have sworn I heard –

A lawn mower?

Must be a mirage, I thought. People lost in the desert imagine they see lakes in the distance. Maybe people freezing in blizzards think they hear lawn mowers. I imagined I heard it coming closer.

Then I imagined I *saw* it. It had a huge yellow eye. This was some mirage!

It was getting really close now – and really weird. The mirage had somebody riding on it. It was going to run us down! I screamed.

Jesse grabbed me. "Stevie! It's a snowmobile!"

What?? I peered through the flying snow.

Jesse stumbled away from the fence and waved both arms. "Here! Here! We're over here."

Spraying snow, the snowmobile slowed and stopped beside us. Its rider looked like something out of a bad dream. A flaming red snowsuit, a black ski mask over its face, and a helmet over its head. It waved us towards the snowmobile.

"Get on!" called a muffled voice.

I didn't have to be asked twice. I clambered on behind the driver and Jesse climbed up behind me. Another roar, and we were off.

Now *this* was better. We were flying over the snow. Dozens – hundreds – of those slow painful steps were being gobbled up by this wonderful machine. This wasn't a mirage. It was a miracle!

"Whoooooeeee!" I yelled. The black head shifted slightly in front of me, and the red-suited body hunched forward.

Wait a minute. Who *was* that masked head?

Suddenly I froze. I mean, froze worse than I was already frozen. A horrible thought hit me. Muffy had a snowmobile. It had been sitting right in front of the garage the night we went to the meeting with Misha.

Could it be *Muffy* under the black mask?

But she was going the wrong way. If it was Muffy, she would turn and head back to her own house. Wouldn't she?

Unless ... maybe she was tricking us. That would be a really Muffy-ish thing to do. I'd never known such a dumb-looking person with so many smart tricks.

Was it Muffy? There was only one way to find out. Taking one hand off the rider's waist, I grabbed the helmet.

CHAPTER

THE SNOWMOBILE SKIDDED – LEFT, RIGHT, LEFT – almost hit the fence, then skimmed to a stop. The head whipped around. I stared into the masked face.

"Who *are* you?" I demanded.

Silence. The helmet came off. Then the mask. Long, dark hair tumbled across the shoulders of the suit. A girl's face, high-cheeked and thin, about fifteen, glowered at me.

"Satisfied?" she said. The wind sent her hair swirling in a floating cloud.

"Yeah, sure."

"Try anything else stupid, and you walk."

"Gotcha," I said quickly, but she was already putting the mask back on.

I gripped her bright red waist gratefully. Whoever she was, she had saved our lives, and there was nowhere on earth I'd rather have been than on the back of her big noisy snowmobile. The high-pitched roar of its motor was as comforting as a lullabye as we zoomed alongside the fence.

Wait a minute. That roar. A little blip went off in my brain – the kind of blip that usually means a brilliant detective insight. I slapped both hands over my mouth. Jesse and I immediately lurched hard to the right.

"STEE-VEEE!" he yelled.

I grabbed the driver's waist again and grinned. I had it! The missing piece of the puzzle. I had figured out *how* Muffy had done it. I turned to tell Jesse, but the wind whipped the words out of my mouth and blew them into the storm.

A minute or two later, the snowmobile slowed down. Just ahead was a break in the fence. Right beside it, a funny little box sat in the snow. Looked like a breadbox.

No. A *mailbox* – the kind that sits on a pole. The pole must have been buried under snow. So this had to be a driveway. The girl turned her snowmobile to the right, and a few seconds later, we could see a light. Above a door.

Attached to a *house!*

To the left was a large picture window, filled with faces, all pressed against the glass. When the people inside saw the snowmobile, they started dancing around, hugging each other.

The girl stopped the snowmobile, leaped off and slogged towards the house. Jesse and I followed. When we reached the door, a bunch of hands dragged us in, pulling off gloves, mitts, boots and parkas, pushing us into easy chairs, piling blankets onto us, and rubbing at our hands and feet.

I closed my eyes and let the hands rub. I heard "frostbite" and "could have frozen to death" and a whole bunch of worried clucks. Also "Stupid, crazy kids!" More than once.

Someone offered to make warm drinks. When I heard the words "hot chocolate," my eyes popped open.

"Er . . . could you make that soup?"

Minutes later, a mug of tomato soup was placed in my hands. Sipping it gratefully, I glanced around.

The red-snowsuit girl was sitting on a couch, wearing jeans now and a blue sweatshirt. She was surrounded by four or five kids who looked a lot like her. A couple of adults you could spot in a second as a mom-and-dad pair were delivering a double-whammied lecture on blizzards. As soon as one stopped to take a breath, the other one started in. After listening for a couple of minutes, I figured out that the girl, who they called Kirsten, had been at a friend's house when the blizzard started. Her friend's parents had told her to stay the night, but she had a new video back home that she wanted to watch. So she got on her snowmobile – cool transportation for a kid, I'd say – and headed home. Good luck for me and Jesse, who just happened to be on her route. Back luck for her, now that her parents had gotten ahold of her.

"A video?" her dad was saying. "You risked your life for a *video?*"

"But I followed the fence, and – "

"Fence?" said her mom. "You thought a *fence* would keep you safe?"

"The fence could have been buried under half a metre of snow!" added her dad.

I was hoping, since Jesse and I were strangers,

that we could maybe stay out of it. Maybe, if we just quietly sipped our soup, they'd forget about us.

Fat chance.

"And who," said the dad-type finally, "are *these* two?" He pointed at me and Jesse.

Kirsten looked relieved. "I have no idea. I saw them hanging over the fence, half dead, so I stopped to pick them up."

Half dead? I sat up straight, insulted. Maybe Jesse was half dead. *I* had merely stopped to think.

The mom-type turned to face us. "I'm Ellie Klassen," she said, "and this is my husband, John, and our kids. Now who exactly are *you?* And why were you draped over our fence in the middle of a blizzard?"

Well, they asked.

It took most of an hour. There was no way we could explain our escape from Muffy's house without telling them about the robbery and Muffy's confession. That made me a little nervous. For all I knew, they were Muffy's best friends.

But the looks Mr. and Mrs. Klassen exchanged told me they weren't crazy about Muffy. "She's made trouble in the neighbourhood for years," said Mr. Klassen.

"Thinks she's better than everyone else," added Mrs. Klassen.

"Still," said Mr. Klassen, scratching his head, "it's one thing not to like her. But a thief?"

As it turned out, the Klassens knew quite a bit about the theft at Muffy's house. *They* were the neighbours who had seen Old Pete drive by on the night of the robbery.

"You mean, *you're* the police witnesses?" said Jesse.

Mr. Klassen nodded. "We felt bad about it because we know Misha Kulniki. He's been here at a couple of Kirsten's birthday parties. Seems like a good boy. But we had to tell the truth. We *did* see his car cruise by – twice."

Mrs. Klassen nodded. "It was the only car we saw all night. It's so quiet on this road that we notice all the cars. Misha's was hard to miss. It was going so slowly I thought something must be wrong. It even pulled into our driveway for a moment – remember, John? I went to the window and waved, but Misha just pulled out again."

"Of course," I said. "Because it wasn't Misha."

Mrs. Klassen frowned.

"It was *Muffy* driving Old Pete that night."

"Muffy?" said Jesse.

I turned to face him. "She wanted to steal the plants, right? But she had to make it look like *someone else* had done it. So on the night of the robbery, she stole Old Pete and drove it up this road. She made sure the Klassens saw the car so they could tell the police. Don't you see? She *framed* Misha so that he'd get blamed."

Kirsten shook her head. "That doesn't make sense. How could Muffy steal Old Pete? She didn't even go out."

Mrs. Klassen nodded. "Kirsten's right. Muffy's Mercedes definitely did not go by."

"She didn't take her *car,*" I agreed.

They all looked confused.

"Her snowmobile! She did the whole thing on her snowmobile."

"What?" squeaked Jesse.

I turned to the Klassens. "I know you didn't see Muffy's car that night, but did you see any snowmobiles?"

"I can't remember," said Mrs. Klassen.

"I can!" said one of the boys. "That was the night the Ewanchucks were out goofing around."

"The Ewanchucks are our neighbours on the other side," explained Mr. Klassen. "Four teenagers. Four snowmobiles. They're roaring up and down here all the time. We try to ignore it."

"You see?" I slapped my hand on a table. "Muffy *knew* she could ride her snowmobile right past your house, and nobody would notice."

"It's true," said Mrs. Klassen, glancing at Mr. Klassen. "We don't even look up anymore when we hear a snowmobile."

"She wouldn't need the road anyway," said Kirsten. "She could have gone over the back fields."

I nodded. "So Muffy rides her snowmobile the ten kilometres to Bobbi's house. Then she hides it – in a ditch or something. She steals Old Pete and drives back here, making sure the Klassens get a good look at the car."

Kirsten was leaning forward, fascinated. "But how could Muffy get Old Pete started?"

"The key was in the glove compartment," Jesse explained. "It always is."

I nodded. "Jesse and I heard Misha blabbing about it. Muffy could easily have found out the same way."

"Okay," said Jesse, drumming his legs with excitement, "so Muffy drives back to her house, steals the plants, takes them somewhere, and then – what?"

"She drives Old Pete back to Bobbi's yard, picks up her snowmobile and drives it home." I shrugged. "Daring but simple."

"And smart!" Jesse shook his head in awe. "She made Misha look totally guilty. And she made herself look totally innocent. Aiii, Stevie, what a plan!"

I nodded. "Behind those blueberry eyes lies the brain of a criminal mastermind. And that's not *all* she planned, Jesse. The break-in at Bobbi's greenhouse on the night we made the trap – remember I heard a lawn mower?"

Jesse blinked. "Muffy's snowmobile?"

I nodded. "She snuck up to Bobbi's house on her snowmobile and then crept up to the greenhouse on foot. That was why we didn't see or hear a car."

"Awesome!" said Jesse.

"She had another trick, too. Knowing she might leave footprints in the snow, she didn't wear her own boots. She wore a larger pair – her ex-husband's, I think – so that even if someone found footprints, they wouldn't suspect her. She wore her shoes inside the big boots to make them fit."

Mr. Klassen shook his head. "Amazing."

"Shocking," agreed Mrs. Klassen.

Kirsten got to her feet. "We'll have to phone the police right away," she said. Then she stopped. "But won't they want some proof?"

Jesse suddenly looked scared. "Proof? Hey, Stevie, do we have any proof?"

I nodded. "That room full of orchids, for starters. Not to mention this envelope." Reaching into my pocket, I pulled out the envelope addressed to the president of the Orchid Society.

Jesse snatched it, read it and grinned. "This is great. It proves that Muffy had a reason to steal those plants."

I nodded. "A motive. Too bad we didn't have time to grab those boots, too. The police could have matched the goo stains on the boot with the stains on your clothes, Jesse. Then they'd know for sure that Muffy was in Bobbi's greenhouse that night."

The littlest Klassen boy crept up to my chair and whispered, "What did the boots look like?"

I stared at him. What difference did it make?

"Light brown," I said, "with a big orange stain on the bottom of one."

He raced out of the room. Seconds later, he ran back in, carrying –

"Jesse, it's them! It's the boots!"

Jesse grabbed them and flipped them upside-down. When he saw the stain, his face split into a grin.

"But how did they get here?"

We both stared at the littlest Klassen.

"You were wearing them when you came in," he said.

"Really? Which one of us?"

"Both of you!"

"*Both* of us?"

Mrs. Klassen grinned. "Davey is right. You were each wearing one of these boots and a different boot that didn't match. We couldn't help but notice."

"We left in a bit of a hurry," I told her. "Not much chance to choose matching outfits."

Jesse was pointing at the stain on the right boot. "Stevie! Here it is. The proof!"

I grinned. The two of us slapped hands.

I was sort of hoping that would be it and we could just phone the police. But being parent-types, the Klassens couldn't resist one last lecture. Jesse and I had been foolish to go out in the blizzard. We could have died if Kirsten hadn't come along. We were lucky not to have lost all our fingers and toes plus a few ears and noses.

It all seemed a bit unfair. Nobody knew better than me and Jesse how close we'd come to winding up frozen in a snowbank, ghastly pioneer grins on our faces. Besides, we would hear this lecture at least two more times – first from Bobbi and then from our parents back in Vancouver.

As soon as it was over, we headed for the phone. The Klassens told us that their phone and electricity had been out for a while, like Muffy's, but had just come on again.

When Bobbi heard Jesse's voice, she squealed so loudly that Jesse jerked the phone away from his ear. He waited till she'd calmed down, then asked about Misha. Listening to Jesse's side of the conversation, I figured out that Misha had gotten snowed-in at the gas station. It sounded like he had gotten pretty hysterical about what had happened to Jesse and me. It sounded, in fact, like everyone was in a huge panic about us.

"The police?" said Jesse. "They're planning a search? What, on snowmobiles? Tell them to come here, Bobbi. We've got a very interesting story to tell them."

Bobbi, of course, had to hear the story herself. Jesse got all excited telling it – so excited that he must have forgotten I was listening. Anyway, I noticed that a few details shifted around a bit.

Like *who* did *what*.

"Yeah, Bobbi, we discovered this room full of orchids in Muffy's house. She's an orchid nut, yes. That's why she was trying to stop the exhibit. I even found an envelope addressed to the president of the Orchid Society. And Bobbi? I've got proof that Muffy broke into your greenhouse. Just before we escaped from her house, I managed to grab her boots! They've got an orange stain from that goo."

A pause.

"Nah, it was nothing. Just regular stuff for a detective."

Another pause.

"No, Bobbi, not really a hero. I just wanted to help Misha, that's all."

Silence. Then, "Stevie? I'll go get – "

Glancing up, he spotted me. It took half a second for his face to turn tomato red. Then he put one hand over the phone. "I guess you, uh, heard."

I nodded.

"She wants to talk to you."

I took the phone. "Bobbi? Hi, it's Stevie. Yeah, we're fine. Yeah, he sure is. Very brave. I agree. Brilliant. Yes, I *know* I'm lucky to be his partner."

I watched a sheepish little grin crawl across Jesse's face.

"Thanks," he said after I hung up.

"It's okay," I said, throwing an arm around his shoulder. "After all, if you can't be a hero to your grandmother, who *can* you be a hero to?"

CHAPTER

"ISN'T THIS GREAT?" I WAVED A CHEESE-AND-CRACKER-filled hand around at the crowded Conservatory. "Aren't you glad we stayed?"

Jesse and I were standing in the best spot – right beside the refreshment table – at the grand opening of the 'Carnivores!' exhibit. We'd had to delay our flight home by two days to be here, but since they'd made us the guests of honour, it hadn't been a hard decision. The place was jammed – members of the Carnivore Club, Conservatory people, City Hall people, reporters, and a whole bunch of school groups. The Klassens, too, and Oliver and his family.

"Sure, I'm glad," said Jesse, taking a tiny sip from his ginger ale. "For Misha, I mean. But these plants still give me the creeps. How can you *eat* in here?"

"I can eat anywhere," I said. Then, remembering Muffy's house, I shivered. "Well, almost anywhere."

Muffy De Witt's career as a plant thief was over. At first, she had tried to deny everything. But when the police showed her the envelope and the stained boot, she totally lost it. She treated the police to the speech about her parents and the Royal Orchid Society and those horrible people in the Carnivore Club. It took the police a bit of time – and a few explanations from Diamond & Kulniki – to straighten it all out, but eventually they knew exactly what had happened. I had been right about her using a snowmobile – even about her hiding it in a ditch. Muffy was now up to her blueberry eyes in trouble.

The police had even gotten the plants back. Muffy had driven them to the home of another member of the Orchid Society, a dim type who had been away for Christmas and who thought, on returning, that the stolen plants were some strange new kind of orchid. She was feeding them special orchid fertilizer to try to make them *bloom*.

In spite of what they'd been through, the plants were okay. They filled every corner of the exhibit with their weird-looking leaves and pitchers and tentacles. The other kids in the crowd looked just as amazed by them as I had been. The exhibit was definitely going to be a hit.

Lester Potts forced his way through the crowd to me and Jesse. "Isn't it wonderful?" he said, spraying cracker crumbs over his shirt in his enthusiasm. "It's like a dream come true."

"Did you hear? Did you hear?" crowed Veda Bickel, looming up behind him. "The permanent carnivorous plant wing is ours. We've done it!"

They grabbed hands and jumped around a little, squealing with excitement. Oh great, now Lester was spraying *me* with cracker crumbs. I backed away.

A strange woman stepped into my place. No, *not* strange. She was actually very familiar. It was the mousy-looking woman with the pinchy nose – the one who had glared at us in the Conservatory cafeteria when Lester was hiding behind his newspaper.

The second Lester saw her, he stopped dead. "Oh dear," he said. "I mean, *my* dear. My dear Harriet! Let me introduce you to our guests of honour. Stevie and Jesse, I'd like you to meet my wife, Harriet Potts."

His wife?

Harriet gave us a mouth-only smile. Then she put her arm firmly through Lester's. "Isn't it time for us to be leaving, Lester? There's a great deal of work to do at the shop."

Lester mumbled as he chewed on a last bit of cracker. Then, with a sad little wave, he left with Harriet.

"Dear old Lester," said Veda with a sigh.

"What's the story?" I asked.

"Harriet thinks he should spend less time on carnivorous plants and more time working on the flowers they sell in their shop. I don't really blame her. Their shop isn't doing all that well. But Lester *does* love his little carnivores so."

"Eeeyuggh!" Jesse shuddered.

Veda didn't notice. Spotting another clump of Carnivore Club members, she stalked off to tell them the good news.

I was checking out the food when I felt a tug on my elbow.

Oliver's little sister, Mary Beth. "Stevie, Jesse, look!" With a loud grunt, she dropped the plastic box she was carrying onto a chair and jerked off the lid. Jesse and I peered inside.

"What is *that?*" asked Jesse.

In the box was a huge, perfectly round ball of fur.

"It's Sigmund!" cried Mary Beth. "We found him! He was hiding behind the hot-water heater."

"Gee," said Jesse, "sure is a big one, isn't he?"

I nodded. I've seen *dogs* that weren't that big.

Mary Beth smiled happily. "Oh, he's grown a lot since he got lost. Must be because of the birdseed."

"Birdseed?" I repeated.

"Oliver spilled a bag of birdseed behind the hot-water heater," Mary Beth explained. "Mom says Sigmund has done nothing but eat since December 17."

Jesse and I peered into the box again.

"Scary," said Jesse.

"*Very* scary," I agreed.

"Come on, Sigmund," said Mary Beth. "Time for your nap."

A nap. Sure. All that eating wears a hamster out.

And speaking of eating ...

The refreshment table was definitely the heart of the action. As soon as Mary Beth disappeared, Oliver showed up, holding hands with his girlfriend, Vanessa. We'd met her the day before.

It was Vanessa who had finally cleared up the mystery of the plants in Oliver's room. It turned out that it wasn't plants, it was *plant*. One plant – a poinsetta Vanessa had given Oliver for Christmas. She had hung little golden hearts all over it, and every one of them had her initials and Oliver's written on it in pink ink. Oliver had looked *very* embarrassed as she described it.

Well, of course, when Vanessa found out Oliver had been keeping her present in a dark basement room with the door locked, she wanted to know why. Oliver had hummed and hawed, blushing madly. Finally he told her it was because he wanted to keep it all to himself. Vanessa actually *believed* him. She even gave him a kiss on the cheek and called him "Snookums," which had made him blush even worse. Lucky for him she hadn't asked where the poinsetta had ended up. Upside-down and frozen stiff in some garbage can was my guess.

"Hi, Vanessa," I said, as the two of them strolled up to us. "Hi, Snookums – uh, Oliver." I couldn't resist.

Jesse laughed. Vanessa smiled. Snookums looked like he was ready to tear my scalp off, one hair at a time.

"Oh, don't be such an old grump," crooned Vanessa. Snookums grinned at her and blushed. The two of them went into Deep Eyelock.

"Eeeyuggh!" muttered Jesse under his breath.

My feelings exactly. If this was flirting, they could have it.

I felt better when I saw Kirsten coming, followed closely by Misha. They were turning into a teenage romance, too, but not the kind that makes you want to throw up. Ever since Kirsten had brought Jesse and me home on her snowmobile, it was obvious that she and Misha really liked each other. But they didn't talk baby talk or draw stupid hearts around their names or give each other Significant Glances. They just acted like they liked each other, that's all.

Simple.

I liked it.

"Hey, Stevie, Jesse! Nice work, kids." Kirsten waved a hand around at the carnivorous plants. "You saved the day. You're heroes."

"You're the *real* hero," I said. "You saved our lives."

She smiled and gave a little shrug. "Listen, guys, we're going to catch a movie tonight – me and Misha and Vanessa and Oliver. Do you two want to come?"

"It'll be fun," chirped Vanessa. "Like – a triple date!"

Date?

Jesse and I stared at each other. He didn't say "Eeeyuggh!" but I could tell he was thinking it. So was I. For a second, I was about to get all weirded out.

But then I thought, hey, this is Jesse. My bud. How could it be a date?

Even if it was, who cared?

"Sure," I said.

"Uh, sure," echoed Jesse. "What's the movie?"

"*Avalanche*," said Kirsten. "It's supposed to be great." She looked around. "Did somebody say there were brownies around here?"

"Down at the other end of the table," said Misha. "I'll be right there. I just want to talk to Stevie. Alone."

Uh, oh.

They all moved off – even Jesse, who was looking awfully curious.

"Listen, Stevie," Misha began. He was glancing around the room and at the floor – everywhere but at me. "I just wanted to say – I'm sorry. I gave you a hard time. And I called you some … well, some really dumb names."

"Pea brain," I said, in case he'd forgotten. "Ditzy. Nut-case."

"I know."

"Looney tune," I added.

"I *know*. I'm trying to apologize. Jesse told me it was you who figured everything out and got Muffy to confess. I … well, I don't understand how detectives work, I guess. You did some pretty strange things. But now I know everything you did had a reason."

"That's right," I said. The dirt-throwing. The falling in his lap. Must have been *some* good reason for all that stuff.

"So I wanted to say I'm sorry – and thanks. If it weren't for you … well, I don't want to think about it."

"That's okay, Misha."

"Friends?" he said, holding out a hand.

"Friends," I said, shaking it.

We were interrupted by the sound of a microphone being tapped and a voice saying, "Testing, testing."

Misha nodded towards the stage on the other side of the Conservatory. "Speech time," he said. "You better get ready to be thanked a lot."

He led the way towards the stage.

Suddenly he stopped. "Listen, Stevie, there's just one thing. The first night you showed up, you seemed to be staring at me a lot. Raising your eyebrows. Making strange faces. I know it had something to do with your detecting, but – what?"

I gulped. "I'd, uh, like to tell you, Misha, really I would. But I can't."

"Why not?"

"Oh, you know."

He shook his head. "No."

"Professional secret," I said.

"Oh." He looked disappointed.

I felt a bit bad. But just a tiny bit.

After all, what's the good of being a detective if you can't keep at least one mystery to yourself?

"… and now I'd like to introduce our first guest of honour, Stevie Diamond."

Winking at Misha, I headed for the stage.

READ THE OTHER BOOKS IN THE STEVIE DIAMOND MYSTERY SERIES:

How Come the Best Clues Are Always in the Garbage?

Stevie and Jesse have a thief to catch. The thousand dollars that belonged to Garbage Busters, an environmental group, is missing — stolen right off the Diamonds' kitchen table.

How Can I Be a Detective If I Have to Baby-sit?

Plans for an exciting vacation at her father's tree-planting camp turn sour when Stevie learns that she's been volunteered to baby-sit the cook's son. That is, until she learns about Rubberface Ragnall.

Who's Got Gertie? And How Can We Get Her Back!

Stevie and Jesse are in the thick of things once again. Gertie, their 72-year-old neighbour, goes missing while they are helping her prepare for a big movie. Suddenly they have a summer project far more exciting than day camp.

ABOUT THE AUTHOR

Linda Bailey grew up in Winnipeg and has fond memories of the Great Blizzard that closed her school for three days. She now lives in Vancouver, where she often gets soggy but rarely gets really cold.